DEAD IS
A KILLER
LLER
TUNE

OTHER BOOKS BY MARLENE PEREZ

Dead Is the New Black

Dead Is a State of Mind

Dead Is So Last Year

Dead Is Just a Rumor

Dead Is Not an Option

Dead Is a Battlefield

The Comeback

Love in the Corner Pocket

DEAD IS A KILLER TUNE

marlene perez

Houghton Mifflin Harcourt

Boston   New York   2012

Library of Congress Cataloging-in-Publication Data
Perez, Marlene.
Dead is a killer tune / Marlene Perez.
p. cm. — (Dead is—)
Summary: Jessica and the other viragos must find who is responsible for the
haunting music that is compelling Nightshade residents to commit crimes.
Can they find out who is "behind the music" before it's too late?
ISBN 978-0-547-60834-1 (pbk.)
[1. Supernatural—Fiction. 2. Music—Fiction. 3. Bands (Music)—Fiction. 4. High
schools—Fiction. 5. Schools—Fiction. 6. Interpersonal relations—Fiction.] I. Title.
PZ7.P4258Dck 2012
[Fic]—dc23
2012014798

To my best friend, Michelle,
who made high school almost bearable.

DEAD IS A KILLER TUNE

CHAPTER ONE

The bad thing about being a virago wasn't the mysterious whirling tattoo, my hard-as-nails trainer Flo, or even that I regularly put my life in danger to keep Nightshade safe.

All of those things I could handle, but what I couldn't handle was arguing with my parents for the thousandth time about why I couldn't watch my little sisters.

My best friend, Eva, had no sympathy. "Why not tell them the truth?" she asked when I called her to complain about their unreasonable attitudes.

"You *have* met my parents, right?" I responded. I couldn't think of two people less likely to believe that werewolves, vampires, and witches lived in Nightshade, or that it was my sworn duty to protect them. Or fight them. It depended upon the day of the week.

A few years ago, my big brother Sean went all furry and my parents didn't even notice.

My mom didn't even blink when Sean started shoveling two-pound slabs of rare meat down his gullet for breakfast, lunch, and dinner.

She just mumbled something about growing boys and then asked me to do the laundry.

Eva had been talking, but I'd missed half of it, probably because I was still thinking about my parents. Or maybe because her pet raven, Poe, was croaking "Nevermore!" in the background.

"Say that last part again," I said.

"I knew mentioning Dominic would get your attention," she replied.

I didn't even bother to deny it. "What about him?"

"I asked if you and Dominic wanted to go out with Evan and me this weekend. There's a VP triple feature."

VP stood for Vincent Price. Eva was a serious horror movie fan.

"I'll ask," I said.

"Your parents or your boyfriend?"

"He's *not* my boyfriend," I insisted. Dominic Gray was the lead singer of Side Effects May Vary — all six foot three, blond, blue eyes, and high cheekbones of him.

We'd gone out a few times, but calling him my boyfriend was definitely premature. Especially since I had the distinct impression he'd been avoiding me lately.

Eva lost interest in the subject of my pathetic love life and hung up a few minutes later.

I stayed by the phone and brooded. Dominic and I had grown closer since we had saved Eva from becoming a brain-munching zombie, but I still sensed some reserve in him.

Maybe it was because I was high-risk as a potential girlfriend. As a virago — a woman warrior — I got hit a lot, and sometimes nasty things wanted to eat me. I'd had a run-in with a hungry chupacabra a few months ago, but it had been quiet in Nightshade since then. Almost too quiet.

When my parents came home and let me off the hook, I headed for the library. I had a new assignment from my guitar teacher. My favorite librarian, Ms. Johns, was working at the reference desk.

"Jessica, I haven't seen you around lately," she greeted me. Ms. Johns had a mass of curly brown hair and a smile that practically made you smile back.

"Hi, Ms. Johns. I was hoping you could help me. Does the library have any sheet music? My guitar teacher wants me to learn a new song and she's letting me choose it."

She pointed me in the right direction, and I spent time thumbing through the selections. Nothing seemed right, though. I hated to part with my precious allowance money, but it looked like I might have to.

Ms. Johns came up as I was leaving. "No luck?" she asked.

"Not really," I said. "I'm looking for something really different."

"I know of an estate sale on Saturday," she said. "Mr. Lindquist played several instruments for years, but he's moving to Florida and is selling almost everything. Maybe you can find something there." She wrote down the address on a piece of paper and handed it to me.

"Thanks for the tip," I said. "See you later."

I liked the idea of performing something unusual, maybe even something my teacher, Ms. Minerva, had never heard before.

Saturday morning, it was foggy and rainy, which didn't make Eva happy.

"Remind me why we had to get up at the crack of dawn?" Eva complained as my mom dropped us off at the estate sale.

I gestured to the dozens of cars already parked in the street in front of the house. "This is why," I told her. "Mr. Lindquist is a serious collector. Musicians from all over California are coming to this sale."

As if to prove my point, a pasty-looking guy in leather pants and a vest without a shirt stepped out of a black town car. He groaned and fumbled for his sunglasses.

I nudged Eva. "He's clearly not used to getting up this early either."

The house was a typical-looking tract home on the outside, with a two-car garage, beige paint, and a manicured lawn. Music notes had been painted on the front door and one of the hedges was in the shape of a saxophone.

A baby grand piano stood in a position of honor in the living room, near a big bay window. Teddie Myles, the owner of the all-ages club the Black Opal, sat at the piano and touched the keys softly. Today, the purple highlights in her hair had been replaced with hot pink and lime green streaks.

On the opposite wall, above a leather couch, hung three guitars. Three amazing guitars. I went to get a closer look.

"Dominic would love this!" I exclaimed, pointing to a Rickenbacker guitar.

"What would I love?" a familiar voice asked.

I whirled around. "I didn't know you were coming."

"Neither did I, until about an hour ago," he replied. "Aunt Katrina wanted to check it out." Dominic and his aunt were both in the band Side Effects May Vary.

Eva said, "I'm going to look for" — long pause while she figured out what to say — "something over there."

After she left, Dominic and I pretended to admire the guitars.

"I called you," I finally said, "about that triple feature tonight."

"I've been meaning to call you back," he said. Another long pause.

"It's okay," I said, even though it wasn't. "I already told Eva no."

"Jessica, I wanted to talk to you about something."

"You have a strange way of showing it."

Harmony and Selena approached before Dominic could tell me whatever it was he wanted to say. Noel and Connor were trailing behind them. The guys were best friends, and I was pretty sure Noel and Harmony were dating. Connor and I had gone out a couple of times, but I broke things off and he'd avoided me ever since.

That apparently hadn't changed because he took one look at me and nudged Noel. "Let's check out the albums in the next room."

"What are you two talking about so intently?" Selena asked.

"Nothing," Dominic said.

"This guitar," I added. I pointed to the purple Fender Stratocaster on the wall.

"Are you going to buy it, Jessica?" Selena asked. "Because if not, it would go perfectly with this outfit I just bought."

Selena didn't even play guitar. She was just being petty. She probably *would* buy it, just because she knew I wanted it.

I glanced at the price tag and nearly gasped out loud. "It's out of my price range," I said, trying to sound cheerful about it. "Excuse me, I think I'll go look for some sheet music." I told myself it wasn't practical anyway. I usually played acoustic guitar, although I had played electric guitar a few times. Ms. Minerva expected us to be well-rounded musically.

I didn't look back at Dominic. He knew where to find me if he really wanted to talk to me.

I found Eva in a room lined with bookcases, full of books, magazines, and even old albums. There were three shelves crammed with nothing but sheet music. I pulled out a stack of music to examine.

A hand-carved flute sat on a stand in the corner.

"Jessica, isn't this cool?" she asked. She pointed to the flute.

"It's beautiful." I picked it up carefully to look for a price tag, but there wasn't one.

"That's not for sale." A small man stepped out of the shadows, leaning on a cane.

I put the flute back on the stand slowly. "I've never seen anything like it," I replied.

"It's made of boxwood with an ivory inlay," he said. "I'm Mr. Lindquist, the owner."

He picked up the flute and took it over to the only chair in the room. He brought the instrument to his lips and played.

There was silence when he finished and then Eva and I broke into spontaneous applause.

"What's all the noise about?" Selena asked from the doorway.

Mr. Lindquist put the flute back in its place. "Just a little practice," he said pleasantly. "Now, if you'll excuse me, I'd better see how the sale is going."

After he left, I gave Selena a dirty look and then returned to the stack of sheet music. I sat down on the floor to go through it. Harmony took a spot near me and started rummaging through another stack.

"I'm starting a band," she said importantly. "We're calling it Magic and Moonlight. I'm going to be the lead singer, of course."

"That's nice," I commented mildly. Harmony's mom was the Nightshade High chorus director, but Harmony couldn't sing a note.

I'd almost made my way through the entire stack

when I found something intriguing. It was a handwritten song, the paper browned by age and frayed at the edges. Just as I reached for it, Harmony snatched it away.

"Hey!" I said. "I was looking at that."

"Finders keepers," Harmony told me. She bounced up and ran over to Selena. "Look," she said. "This will be perfect for our band."

"Whatever," I muttered, and returned to my stack.

Eva and I ignored them until they finally left.

"What's with Selena lately?" Eva asked.

I shrugged. "She's been hanging out with Harmony a lot, ever since she and Dominic broke up."

"I wouldn't exactly call it a breakup," Eva replied. "You can't count it as a relationship if you had to use magic to get the guy to like you in the first place."

I didn't want to talk about Dominic anymore. Eva seemed to sense my reluctance and changed the subject. "Let's find you some sheet music," she said.

I found a couple of great song possibilities and put them in my to-buy stack.

"Did you see anything else you like?" Eva asked me. She was being a good sport about following me around. Eva wasn't a huge music person, like me — she was into horror movies and her boyfriend Evan, in that order, but

Evan didn't seem to mind. He was almost as much of a horror buff as Eva was.

"That purple guitar," I said. "But it's completely out of my price range. Selena probably bought it already anyway."

"My mom says that at estate sales, price is negotiable," Eva said. "Let's go negotiate."

I got to my feet. "It's worth a try."

But when we went back to look for it, all three of the guitars were gone. "It was too expensive anyway."

Eva gave me a knowing look. "But you still wanted it."

I nodded. "More than you know." We spent a few more minutes wandering around, but I didn't find anything else I wanted and could afford. Maybe babysitting my little sisters wasn't such a bad idea after all. It definitely paid better than being a virago.

"Did you find anything?" I asked Eva.

"Some cool seventies band posters," she said. "I thought I might use them in my horror film." Eva had been talking about filming her own horror movie, and her closet was filled with all sorts of props.

We were standing in line to pay when Selena and Harmony left with Harmony's mom. They carried a couple of huge packages. One was shaped like a guitar.

"They got the sheet music and a guitar," I pointed out to Eva.

"But not the talent," Eva replied. Her dimples flashed as she giggled.

We heard gasps behind us and turned around to see Mr. Lindquist staggering, clutching his head. "My priceless flute has been stolen. Don't let anybody leave!"

His face was pasty and gray. I grabbed a folding chair and led him to it. "Somebody get him some water."

He put his face in his hands. "Gone," he moaned. "It's gone."

"What happened?" I asked.

"I heard the most beautiful music," he said dreamily. "A guitar, I think. And then I must have fallen asleep. When I woke up, the flute was gone."

The police arrived and Chief Wells started barking orders. The chief was new in town. She'd been hired to replace Chief Mendez, even though everyone knew it couldn't be done. At least not in the way that counted.

Eva nudged me and whispered, "Didn't you sense danger? Your swirly tattoo?"

"It's a whirlwind," I answered, "not a burglar alarm. It only warns me of serious danger to the city of Nightshade." Every virago had a whirlwind tattoo like mine.

The police searched the entire house and every single person at the estate sale, but they didn't find the flute.

"You're free to leave," Officer Denton told us. I

remembered the sheet music I still had in my hand and went to pay.

"Poor Mr. Lindquist," I said.

"Poor? Even without that flute, he's worth a fortune," the cashier told me. She handed me my change. "It's a shame about that flute, though. It's a one of a kind from Germany." She leaned in closer to make sure no one could hear her. "In fact, some people even say that it belonged to the Pied Piper of Hamelin."

"You mean the creepy guy who lured all those kids away with music? No way. That's just a myth."

"I'm serious," she replied.

"Mr. Lindquist played the flute today," I said. "And not a thing happened to us."

She shrugged. "I'm only telling you what I heard."

On the way home, Eva and I talked about the theft and the cashier's strange comment.

"I don't believe it for a minute," I said. "She was just trying to scare us."

"I don't know," Eva said. "This *is* Nightshade."

She had a point.

CHAPTER TWO

Katie and Mom were the only ones at home by the time I got back. Mom was on the phone, but she hung up as soon as she saw me.

"Jessica, what took you so long?" Mom scolded. "You promised you'd watch your sister. I was trying to reach Poppy to see if she could cover for you."

"I'm sorry, Mom," I replied. "I completely forgot. There was a robbery and —"

Mom interrupted me. "A robbery? At the estate sale? You're kidding."

"A valuable flute was stolen, but nobody was hurt," I explained.

"That's a relief," she said, and then looked at her watch. "I want to hear all about it, but I'm late."

My mom was a real estate broker and she was always busy on the weekends. I assumed that Dad was off with my five other sisters somewhere. My brother Sean was at college in Orange County.

Mom hurried off, and then Katie asked, "What are we going to do today?"

"Chores first," I said firmly. "Mom left a list." Katie's chore was simple, at least in theory. She had to clean her side of the bedroom she shared with Kellie. Their room was a pit of toys, but we had it straightened up within a few minutes. The doorbell rang as Katie picked up the last stuffed animal.

Samantha Devereaux stood on our doorstep like Katie's personal genie.

"I was in the neighborhood and thought Katie might want to come to Slim's with me for an ice cream," Samantha said. Sam was Sean's girlfriend. Sometimes she still spent time with my family even though he was away at school.

"Can we?" Katie asked. She was six years old, and obsessed with Samantha.

"Of course, you're invited too, Jessica," Samantha added. We didn't get along that well, but I had to give Sam credit: she tried.

"Great," I said. I almost meant it.

Sam had the top down on her red VW convertible, and the wind in my hair cheered me up. Things always looked better when you were in a convertible.

Slim's was an old-fashioned diner with red leather booths, a jukebox, and shiny stainless steel counters. It was also where Flo, my snarky virago trainer, worked as an indifferent server. Her brother owned the place, which probably meant he couldn't fire her. Even if he wanted to.

We grabbed a table and I waved to Flo, who was perched on her usual stool at the counter. Her T-shirt read HI, I'M AN EVIL GENIUS AND I'LL BE YOUR SERVER TODAY.

We ordered three shakes. "Jessica, can I have some money for the jukebox?" Katie asked.

I slid some quarters across the table at her. "Have fun."

Sam and I watched Katie skip to the jukebox. There were dark circles under Samantha's eyes.

"How's college life?" Sam attended UC Nightshade, which meant she was right here in town.

She smiled. "Surprisingly, I love it. I miss Sean, though."

My attention wandered when Dominic and his sister Raven walked in.

"Jessica!" Raven didn't wait for her brother before she slid into the booth next to us. "What are you doing here?"

"The same thing we are, Raven," Dominic said dryly. He fixed his blue eyes on me. "Hello, Jessica. Find anything you liked at the estate sale?"

"Not really," I said stiffly. Then I realized that I hadn't

introduced everyone, so I did. Samantha didn't even pretend she wasn't curious about Dominic.

"Are you guys new to Nightshade?" she asked.

"Dominic is the new lead singer in Side Effects May Vary," I said. "Haven't you been to the Black Opal lately?" Sam and Sean used to frequent the all-ages club when they were in high school.

She shook her head. "I've been busy with school."

Flo walked up with a bunch of to-go bags. "Here's your order." She handed the food to Dominic.

Raven was chatty for a change, but I wondered if it was to make up for her brother's silence. Dominic hardly said a word the entire time, and once, when our knees bumped accidentally, he looked appalled. It was clear he couldn't wait to get away from me.

I needed to talk to Flo anyway. "Excuse me," I said, squeezing out of the booth. Samantha gave me an odd look, but thankfully didn't comment.

I approached Flo, who was back at her perch at the counter. "What's up, Jessica?" she asked. She lowered her voice. "Is this virago business?"

I nodded and filled her in on what had happened at the estate sale.

She frowned. "My tattoo didn't tingle either, so it could have just been a plain old robbery," she said. "But we'll stay alert for any new developments. Thanks, Jessica."

I returned to the table, where Raven was still rambling on.

"Raven," I said, interrupting her in mid-chat, "your food's getting cold."

Dominic stood up abruptly. "We'd better go before Aunt Katrina's meal is ruined."

"She ordered a salad," Raven protested, but Dominic was already halfway out the door. "See you tomorrow, Jessica. Nice to meet you, Sam." Raven gave me an apologetic look and followed her brother out the door.

"Guy problems?" Sam asked.

"Is it that obvious?" I replied. My brother's girlfriend could be a pain in the butt and it killed me to ask her for advice, but I was desperate.

"To an expert like me? Yes," she told me. "How long have you guys been going out?"

"That's the problem," I said. "We're not."

"Bad breakup, huh?"

"I wish," I said.

She laughed. "You *wish* you had a bad breakup? That's different."

"You have to go out with someone on a regular basis before you can break up with him," I replied. "We never got that far."

I found myself telling Sam all about what had happened with Dominic in the fall—everything except me being a virago, of course.

"He's afraid," she finally said, when I ran out of breath.

"Maybe," I admitted. "Lately, it seems like he can barely stand to be in the same room with me."

"So something about you has him scared," she said. "What could that be, I wonder?"

"I have no idea," I said, but it didn't sound convincing.

"Drink your shake," she said. "Things always look better after one of Slim's shakes."

As I slurped my chocolate deliciousness, I wondered if Sam was right. Dominic's mother was a virago too, and she'd basically left them in Nightshade with their Aunt Katrina. No wonder he was leery of dating a virago.

"What if I know what he's afraid of and it's something I can't change?" I asked Sam.

"Then you have two choices," she said. "You can accept that it's never going to happen and move on, or you can fight for him."

Being a virago was something I couldn't change and it was the one thing I knew Dominic had a hard time with. It looked as though Dominic and I didn't stand a chance.

There were plenty of nice guys out there. I told myself I'd find someone else, eventually, but I wasn't sure I believed it.

Katie came back, her face gleaming with the effort it

took to contain her glee. Sam and I exchanged an amused glance.

"What's up, Katie?" I asked.

The "Happy Birthday" song, the one they always sang on her favorite television show, came on.

"Happy birthday, Jessica," Katie said.

"I didn't know it was your birthday today," Sam said. She grinned at Katie as she danced around the table to the music.

"It's not," I whispered. "It's a week away." I hesitated and then added, "I don't suppose you want to come to my birthday party next weekend? It's just cake and ice cream at the house."

"I'd love to," she said. She gave me a smile that made me realize why Samantha had been the most popular girl in high school. Her smile could charm anyone into liking her. Even me.

Sam's dad was in jail and her mom was a permanent no-show. I realized that Sam was probably lonely. It wouldn't kill me to be a little nicer to her.

CHAPTER THREE

Monday at school, I saw Connor in the hallway before first period, talking to Selena and Harmony. A couple of freshman girls watched him from the safety of their lockers.

There was something different about Connor, but it wasn't until chorus after school that I realized what it was.

He was dressed differently. Gone were his serviceable T-shirts and generic blue jeans. Instead, he wore a pair of tight stovepipe jeans and a stylish shirt that clung to his suddenly muscular arms.

I wasn't the only one who had noticed. The girls in chorus were definitely checking Connor out too. His usual smile was absent, but that didn't stop the flirty glances being sent his way.

I looked away and caught Dominic staring at me. I pretended to be fascinated by my shoes, which seemed like the safest thing to do at the moment.

I went to find a place to sit and noticed my favorite librarian, Ms. Johns, sitting in the back of the room with my guitar teacher, Ms. Minerva. I waved to them.

"I wonder what they're doing here," I said to Eva.

"Let's get started," Ms. Clare said. She was our choir director. She always wore a frown and her hair in a tight bun. "I am auditioning today for the closing solo for our spring performance. Who would like to try out?"

Dominic, Harmony, and Connor all raised their hands.

Connor went first.

"I didn't know he could sing," Eva whispered as he walked up to the microphone.

"He *is* in chorus," I pointed out.

"Anybody can sing well enough to get through chorus," she replied. "Look at you."

I raised my eyebrow. "Thanks a lot."

She nudged me. "You know what I mean."

I raised a finger to my lips. "Shh, he's starting."

That was the last thing I said. Connor's voice was amazing — deep and strong with a little bit of a husky Tom Waits thing about it.

Dominic went next. He looked and sounded as gorgeous as ever, and I had to force myself not to melt into his smile when our eyes met. But it was his stage smile, the one he gave everybody, so I pretended to be fascinated with the wall behind him until his gaze landed on someone else.

But the shocker was Harmony. After a brief nervous glance at Selena, Harmony stepped up to the microphone like she owned it. A voice of raw talent came out of her mouth. She sounded like a young Etta James.

"She's hitting the notes!" Eva said. "All the notes."

"She sounds amazing," I said. "What a difference." Harmony, despite her name, had never been able to sing on key before.

Ms. Clare gave us a ten-minute break, and Connor and Dominic were both surrounded by admirers.

"When did Connor become so spicy hot?" Eva asked.

I snapped my fingers. "Snap out of it, Eva," I said. "Remember what happened the last time you got a crush on a guy?"

"Being a zombie wasn't so bad."

"You weren't a zombie," I reminded her. "Just zombielike."

"Close enough," she said cheerfully. "But you're right. Besides, I've already got my own spicy hot boyfriend." She gave Evan a little wave and he came over immediately.

Evan and Eva held hands and talked horror flicks while I watched Connor being swarmed by chorus girls.

Ms. Clare clapped her hands. "Break's over, people. Before we get started again, I would like to introduce my co-chairs for Nightshade's first Battle of the Bands. Please welcome Ms. Johns and Ms. Minerva."

Ms. Minerva went first. "The Battle of the Bands is a month-long event, sponsored by a major music label, as well as Nightshade merchants and the library. Competitors will compete in an initial round. If they do not meet the minimum score requirement, they will be eliminated from the competition. The judges will pick three finalists and then whittle the field down to one grand-prize winner."

She spent more time going over specifics and then Ms. Johns took over. "We want you guys to have fun," she said. "I will be passing around guidelines and a sign-up sheet. We are also looking for volunteers to help with the event. Now I would be happy to answer any questions."

A bunch of hands went up, including mine. "What's the prize?" Connor asked.

"Nightshade merchants are donating various prizes," Ms. Johns said. "But the grand-prize winner will get a cash award and a recording contract with Cranky Kitten Records."

When they'd finished speaking, we clapped politely.

As soon as they left, everyone began to talk at once. People were commenting on Connor's new look as much as they were about the Battle of the Bands. It wasn't just the new clothes. His arms were bigger, his voice was deeper, but his smile was noticeably absent. Despite all the attention he was getting, he didn't look happy. Something had changed in Connor, inside and out, and I wanted to know what it was.

CHAPTER FOUR

Eva had begged me to train with her. I assumed she wanted to stay in shape now that soccer season was over. I decided to start her out with an early-morning run before school on Wednesday.

I ran to her house to pick her up. I knocked on her window, but there was no answer. Finally, I dialed her cell.

Her sleepy voice answered on the third ring. "Hello?"

"Weren't we supposed to be running this morning?" I asked. "I'm outside."

"Come to the front door, but do not ring the doorbell," she said through a yawn. "Bethany would freak if you woke her up this early."

"I can take a rain check," I offered.

"No! I can be ready in ten minutes," she said.

She met me at her door and we tiptoed past her sister Bethany's room to Eva's bedroom.

"Nevermore," Poe squawked. He tried to take a bite out of me through his cage.

Eva shushed him by stroking his glossy black feathers.

"That bird doesn't like me," I said.

"He doesn't like anyone," she told me. "Except me." Eva had adopted the bird after we'd solved a mystery involving Poe's owner. She said he was the perfect pet for a future horror film director.

While Eva got ready, I amused myself by dressing her stuffed teddy bear, Ted Vicious, in his punk rock outfits.

Her ten minutes was more like half an hour, but we finally made it out the door.

"Are you sure you want to do this?" I asked her as we stretched.

"What? You don't think I can keep up with you?" As we talked, she flipped over on her back and stretched her toes all the way over her head.

"I didn't know you could do that," I said.

"You don't know everything about me," she replied. I stared at her. "Okay, you do. I'll admit it, I've been practicing."

"Practicing? Why?"

"It's obvious. If you're going to be a kick-butt virago, I'll be your sidekick," she said. "And I need to be in shape. I don't want a chupacabra to take a bite out of me." She clapped a hand over her mouth. "Sorry! I know that's a touchy subject."

"Not for me," I reassured her. "It's only Dominic that got all freaked out about it."

Right before Halloween, Flo had to take me to the emergency room for stitches after I tangled with a chupacabra and lost.

"Is that why he's been avoiding you?" Eva asked.

"Probably," I admitted. I gave her my hand to help her up. "Let's go."

We ran around the park twice before Eva said anything else. "What's with all the people here?"

I glanced around. She was right. There were people everywhere, many more than there usually were in the park at this hour. A bunch of them wore T-shirts that read HAMLIN across the back.

Eva stopped running. I jogged in place beside her.

"What's Hamlin?" Eva asked.

A guy playing with a crocheted Hacky Sack heard her. "Only the best band there is," he said. "They're playing the Battle of the Bands in Nightshade all month, so here we are."

"You mean you follow the band wherever they go?" I asked.

He nodded. "I've traveled with them for the last six months."

"Where do you stay?" I asked.

He shrugged. "Wherever," he said. "Sometimes we sleep in my van. Sometimes we camp out. They play, we follow."

A thin blonde with a daisy chain in her hair came up and handed us a flier. It read: *Hamlin. You'll follow them anywhere.* There was a sketch of a guy playing a guitar and a long line of people dancing to his tune.

Eva stuffed it in her hoodie and we continued with our run.

We passed several more Hamlin fans. There was one guy playing a recorder and another who played an acoustic guitar. Badly.

"That reminds me, have they caught the person who stole Mr. Lindquist's flute?" Eva asked.

"I haven't heard anything," I replied.

"Let's take a break," Eva said. She pointed to a bench. As we collapsed on the wooden seat, there was a rustling in the tall decorative grass behind us. Someone let out a low moan.

"Stay here," I ordered, and ran in the direction of the sound. Eva ignored me and followed right behind me.

Scotty Turntable, who played in a local band called Drew Barrymore's Boyfriends, wandered out of the brush, a dreamy expression on his face. "That song," he said. "Yes, yes."

Eva and I exchanged puzzled glances, but then my cell buzzed.

A text from Dominic. *Last night, I sang a Naked Eyes song while @ band practice. I think it might be prophetic. Promises, Promises? Make sense to you?*

Maybe, I sent back. *Thanks.*

"Who was that from?" Eva asked curiously.

"Dominic," I replied.

"Oh, so now it's back on?" she said.

I shook my head. "He had one of those episodes where he broke into a random song." Dominic was a seer, who often provided clues through song. Unfortunately, it often interfered with his real singing career.

I looked around the park. It couldn't be a coincidence that a flute supposedly belonging to the Pied Piper was stolen and then a band called Hamlin showed up. I couldn't figure out what it all meant, though.

CHAPTER FIVE

Flo called me after school on Friday and ordered me to help clean out the Mason house, where we often had virago practice. The place belonged to Natalie Mason, who was engaged to Flo's brother, Slim.

"Vinnie's got his band pitching in, and I expect the other viragos to help too," she said. "A bunch of people who are in town for the Battle have no place to stay. They were at the Wilder estate, but the pipes burst, so they're moving to the Mason house."

"Nobody's lived there since Mrs. Mason died," I said. Natalie's grandmother had owned the house. She'd been an old witch. Literally. "There's probably tons of work to do."

"There is," Flo said. "Only one of the rooms is ready right now. My friend will be staying in that one."

"Is she a virago?" I asked.

"*He* is a guy I went to high school with," Flo replied. "Not everyone I know is a virago."

I'd actually never seen Flo with anyone besides her boyfriend Vinnie. And the other viragos, of course. I wondered what she was like when she was in high school.

I agreed to meet her at the Mason house and ran downstairs to tell Mom.

"That's very nice, dear," Mom said. "Take your sisters."

"All of them?" I was horrified by the thought.

"Of course not," Mom replied. "Just Katie and Kellie. I'll drop you off on my way and I'll call you when I can pick them up."

"What time is that going to be?" I asked.

"Around dinnertime," she said firmly. "Dad has to take the rest of the girls to their activities and I have a house to show."

"They have to wear old clothes," I said. "We're cleaning out years of stuff."

Katie and Kellie were thrilled—especially Katie. "Is Dominic going to be there?" she asked when we were on our way to the Mason house.

I hoped not, but instead of saying that, I shrugged and said, "Maybe."

Volunteers were arriving when Mom dropped us off, including Katrina, Raven, and Dominic.

"I guess that answers your question, Katie," I said. She squealed and ran off to say hello. Kellie stayed by my side and held my hand. Katie skipped back to us and grabbed my other hand.

Natalie Mason was unlocking the front door when we walked up. Flo, Vinnie, and Slim were beside her. Slim wore an enormous trench coat and beat-up fedora. "It's dusty in there," he explained.

"Wonderful," muttered Andy. She stepped up onto the porch. "I can't wait to defeat some dust bunnies."

Flo shot her a dirty look. Andy was usually Flo's favorite virago in training so I couldn't help but feel a little satisfied to see her reprimanded.

"I brought extra hands," I said, holding up my sisters' hands entwined in mine.

"Great," Natalie said. "How about a cookie?" She offered the box to my sisters.

"Sorry," I whispered to Flo, "but I couldn't get out of the house without them."

"It's okay," she said. "Just keep them out of trouble. You and Andy can tackle the attic."

Katie tugged on Flo's arm. I've never seen Flo look more scared than when an actual child touched her. "Can Dominic and Raven come with us?"

Sure," Natalie said. "It is a big attic."

Flo nodded and edged away from Katie. Raven and I tried not to giggle. "Okay," Flo said. "Vinnie and I will work on the upstairs bedrooms."

Natalie handed Kellie and Katie a couple of cookies. "The girls can stay here with me for a little while. I'll bring them upstairs after they've eaten."

She reassured us that the entire attic was fully finished, but cluttered. It was a relief, because Mom would kill me if either of my sisters got hurt.

We walked up the narrow steps to the attic. I heard a rustling sound and froze.

"Rats?" Andy moaned.

"If so, that's one big rat," Dominic commented. He pulled on a chain and the light flickered on. The attic was stuffed full of trash and treasures, with boxes covered with years of dust. I expected that, but I didn't expect to see someone else already up there.

A figure holding a flashlight was rummaging through a steamer trunk. I didn't wait for explanations. He was trespassing. I gave him a quick chop to the neck and he crumpled to the ground.

Footsteps pounded up the stairs. "What's going on?" Flo asked.

"We found him searching the attic," Dominic explained.

The man groaned and put a hand to his neck. "What happened?"

"Hunter?" Flo asked. "What are you doing here already?"

He gave her a wry grin and stood. "You invited me, remember?" I caught a closer look at him. He was tall, with perfect blond hair, and wore jeans and a designer shirt that had been expertly tailored to mold to his thin frame. Not exactly rummaging-in-the-attic attire.

His clothes made me feel like a total yokel. I wore washed-out sweats and my mom's old Bush T-shirt, and my hair was in a couple of braids. My Chuck Taylors had not one but two holes in the toes.

"How did you get in?" I asked.

"The place was unlocked when I got here," he said.

Interesting, since I'd just watched Natalie unlocking the door.

He walked over to me and held out a hand. "No hard feelings?" There were strange indigo blue smudges on his hand, but I shook it anyway.

"None," I said.

"Hunter Verrat is one of the best songwriters in the U.S., maybe even in the world," Flo told us. She gave him a hug. "He did me a huge favor by agreeing to be one of the judges for the Battle of the Bands."

"Who else will be staying here?" I asked.

"Talulah Crank, who owns Cranky Kitten Records," Flo said. "And Mitch Peverell, a big music agent."

"We should get started clearing out the clutter then,"

Dominic said. He didn't seem particularly interested in the news that a talent agent was in town.

"You're right," Flo said. "Hunter, I'll show you your room."

They left the attic, but not before Hunter gave a longing look at the trunk he'd been rummaging in when we'd found him.

I stared after them for a long time. "Wonder what he was really doing up here?" I asked.

"Why would he want any of this?" Raven said, gesturing to a box of ratty old Halloween decorations, which was next to a pile of old clothes. She lost interest in the subject and began to sort through a box of fusty knick-knacks.

"He wants something," Dominic said.

"What do you think he was looking for?" I asked. I crossed to the approximate location where we'd found him and opened the steamer trunk.

A delicate porcelain box with its lid askew lay at the bottom of the trunk. A fine indigo powder spilled out of the box. It matched the stains on Hunter's hand.

I didn't want to touch it, but I didn't want to leave it there for him to find again. I didn't know why, but I'd taken an instant dislike to Flo's friend. Maybe because he'd lied to our faces.

There were plenty of hiding places in the attic, but I wanted to find the least likely spot.

"What did you find?" Dominic asked.

"I'm not sure, but it's something." I grabbed a stack of yellowing newspapers and wrapped the container carefully in a few sheets. There was a dollhouse castle in one corner that was taller than I was.

I peered inside. A medieval family of dolls sat abandoned in the kitchen, so I placed the bundle inside one of the tiny bedrooms on the third floor of the castle.

"Natalie should look through some of this stuff," Andy said. "It could be valuable or she might want to keep some of it for sentimental reasons."

"Good idea," I said. "Let's sort it into three piles: one to throw away, one for recycling, and one for Natalie to look at."

We worked for a couple of hours and then Andy suggested a break. We went downstairs, and Natalie, Kellie, and Katie came into the living room, carrying a pitcher of iced tea.

"That looks delicious," I said.

"I grow the mint in the back garden," Natalie said. Vinnie and Flo wandered in holding hands. I thought she'd tell us to get back to work, but instead she said, "I see we all had the same idea about taking a break. The second bedroom is almost finished."

"We're almost finished with our bedroom too," Natalie said. "Jessica, your sisters have been a big help." I poured drinks and Kellie and Katie handed them out to everyone.

The doorbell rang and Natalie went to answer it. She came back accompanied by a tall woman with short, choppy black hair and green eyes. She carried a large black bag in one hand and a laptop in the other.

"This is Talulah Crank," Natalie said. "The owner of Cranky Kitten Records. She'll be staying here once we're all finished cleaning it."

Talulah didn't wait to hear our names. "Thanks for taking me in," she said, dropping her bags. "I've got a dinner meeting, so I'm going to get going."

She followed Natalie out of the room without acknowledging us.

"If she's one of the judges, our band doesn't stand a chance," Dominic said. "She was frosty."

"She's probably just tired," I said.

But the remaining guest was prickly too. We were back in the attic cleaning when we heard a man downstairs bark, "Don't touch that!" Shortly after that, a door slammed.

Dominic, who had been downstairs getting trash bags, returned to the attic with an offended expression on his face. He told us that he had seen the talent agent, Mitch Peverell, arriving with a pile of designer suitcases.

"I just offered to help him," Dominic told us, "but the guy practically bit my head off."

"I wonder why he was so sensitive," Raven said.

Dominic shrugged. "He said there was some confidential paperwork in there. As if I have any interest in that. He went straight to his room."

All three guests had behaved oddly, but maybe it was just part of being in the entertainment business.

I did a check on the kid sisters and saw that they had found the dollhouse.

"Look at this, Jessica," Katie breathed.

"Katie, Kellie, get away from there," I said. My voice was sharp with anxiety.

"Can I play with it?" Katie begged. "Please?"

"You can have it," Natalie said. "If it's okay with your parents, that is."

I tried to protest over the girls' squeals of delight, but I was overruled.

"Are you sure you don't mind?" I finally asked her.

"I'd love for them to have it," she said. "It was my grandmother's, but I was never allowed to play with it. I'll be happy if I never have to see it again."

Flo and Hunter came back to the attic and I shot Dominic a meaningful look.

"Returned to the scene of the crime?" I asked, trying to sound like I was kidding, but meaning it sincerely.

Flo gave me a look and I shut up quickly.

"We came to see if you needed any help," Hunter said. He kept his smile in place, but his eyes scanned the attic. They came to rest on my sisters' new toy. I cringed when I saw a smudge of blue on the front door of the dollhouse.

I was sure Hunter had spotted it too. His eyes narrowed. "That's an interesting piece," he said. "How much would you take for it, Natalie?"

"I'm sorry, but it's Katie and Kellie's," she replied.

Katie stood in front of it protectively. "Can we take it home now, Jessica?"

"I'll give you a hundred dollars," Hunter said. He ignored Natalie's frown and my sister's adamant shake of her head. "Two hundred."

Katie looked ready to cry. "I wish someone would get a life," I muttered under my breath.

"I gave it to Katie and Kellie," Natalie said in a subject-closed voice.

Hunter finally took the hint and quit harassing my sisters.

"We'll take it to your house," Dominic said.

"Now?" Katie asked. "Can we go now?"

"That's a great idea," Dominic said. He picked it up and carried it down the stairs. My sisters followed close behind.

"We'll be right back," I said.

"Don't be gone long," Flo said sternly. It was an order, and I knew I'd better follow it or I'd be running suicides uphill for the next month.

We put the dollhouse in the trunk of Dominic's car, an older black Honda.

"I didn't know you had a car," I commented as we started off.

"I just bought it," he said. I noticed he was a good driver.

When we got to our house, nobody else was home.

"I want to clean up the dollhouse first," I said. "So let's put it in my room for now." Besides, Katie and Kellie shared a room and it was always a mess. Like messier than Eva's room, and she'd been collecting props for a future horror movie since sixth grade.

I needed to move the box with the indigo powder somewhere else, but the dollhouse could use a dusting. I grabbed a Ziploc bag from the kitchen. I didn't want that weird powder getting all over the place. My mom would kill me, and besides, I didn't know what it was. Natalie's grandmother had been a very powerful witch.

Katie and Kellie hung out downstairs while Dominic and I hauled the dollhouse to my room. I grabbed the small porcelain box, but a little spilled out and rained down on the dolls on the first level.

"I'll have to clean it up later," I said. I looked around my room for a place to hide the box and finally settled on my soccer bag.

I rounded up the girls and we headed back to Natalie's house. As soon as we opened the door, the smell of food led us straight to the kitchen.

"Slim's cooking," I said. My stomach gurgled loudly and Kellie giggled.

"I'm hungry," Katie said.

"It is dinnertime," said Dominic. "Let's see what's on the menu."

Mom was supposed to pick up the girls soon. I checked my cell phone guiltily, but there weren't any messages.

"Looks like Mom's running late," I said. Kellie ran to the kitchen and Katie followed her.

"Flo's going to kill me," I said. "She hates kids."

"I'll help keep an eye on them," Dominic said easily.

Natalie and Slim were serving up soup and sandwiches. Hunter was gone, but some of the other members of Side Effects May Vary had shown up. Everyone but their guitarist, Jeff Cool, was in a good mood.

Flo and her boyfriend Vinnie, the drummer, were cuddling at one end of the table.

"How am I supposed to eat with you two making me sick?" Jeff asked in a whiny voice. Flo shoved a sandwich in his mouth.

"Chew," she said.

We were just finishing dinner when Mom showed up. After we said our goodbyes, Dominic, Raven, Andy, and I headed to the attic and got back to work.

We'd been working over an hour when Raven found a cardboard box in the corner. "Come look at this stuff," she said.

The box contained a candelabra with black candles, what looked like the skull of a rat or other small rodent, a sharp knife with an ornate handle, and bundles of strange-smelling herbs.

"It's like something out of a Vincent Price movie," I said.

"Natalie definitely needs to look at this stuff," Andy said. As much as I would have loved for Eva to have it for her prop collection, I agreed. We put the lid back on the box and took the box to the Natalie pile.

Slim came upstairs a few hours later. "You've made a lot of progress," he commented.

"We found a few unusual items," I said. "Including

something we think Natalie should look at." I pointed to the box and he looked inside.

"Tools of dark magic," he said. "We need to get rid of this."

Dominic and I looked at each other. Was that what Hunter had been looking for?

When I got home, I was way too tired to even think about cleaning out the dollhouse.

I grabbed a quick shower and then collapsed into bed.

As I fell asleep, it sounded like someone was playing a tiny piano. It was barely audible, tinny and far away, so I told myself I was already dreaming.

CHAPTER SIX

Even though it was my birthday, I reported to virago training just after sunrise on Saturday.

Everyone else was already gathered in the park when I arrived. We were practicing there to stay out of the way of the guests at the Mason house. But at the park, we had to dodge Hamlin fans and their makeshift campsites. Nightshade was filled to capacity.

During our run, Andy kept trying to pass me. I finally let her. She gave a loud victory crow as we reached our unofficial stopping place in the park. We all dropped to the ground under the shade of an old oak.

"It seems like all we have been doing is running," Raven said. "Flo, can we do something different next week?"

Andy nudged her. "Be careful what you wish for."

Flo cracked a rare smile. "I'll make sure to plan something interesting for our next workout."

"That sounds ominous," I said. And I meant it.

After practice, Flo brought out cupcakes and they sang "Happy Birthday" to me.

"What are you doing for your birthday?" Raven asked. She licked the chocolate frosting off her cupcake.

"Same old thing," I told her. "Dinner with my family." I took a bite of my cupcake. "These cupcakes are good, Flo."

"Slim made them," she said. "He says happy birthday, by the way."

When I got home, I was tired and sweaty. Katie met me at the door. "Jessica, we got your cake," she said.

"That's nice," I said. "I'm going to go take a shower."

"Don't you want to take a look at it?"

Sarah came up behind Katie. "A shower is a good idea." She held her nose.

"Funny," I said.

"But I want to show Jessica her cake," Katie said.

"Not now, pipsqueak," Sarah said. She was in eighth grade and thought she was quite the mature teenager.

Her bossiness made me contrary. "It's my cake," I said. "I'll look at it if I want." I ran into the kitchen and to the fridge, but Sarah beat me to it.

She stepped in front of the refrigerator. "I'm under strict orders. No peeking."

"What's wrong with it?" I demanded.

"There's nothing wrong with your cake," she said. But

when she saw I wasn't going to budge, she added, "It's a surprise. Now go take your shower."

"Okay," I said. Mom had probably gone all out and ordered something different besides the white cake with fresh strawberries and whipped cream. It had been my favorite when I was five, and she'd ordered it for every one of my birthdays since.

Somehow, the idea made me happy. Maybe this birthday would be different, I thought, as I headed upstairs. I didn't know how different it would be.

Mom came into my bedroom after I got out of the shower. "Jessica, Eva's here and we're ready to cut the cake."

"Why didn't she come up?" I asked.

"Uh, Katie wanted to show her the cake," Mom said. She gave my ratty old sweats the eye. "Is that what you're wearing?"

"It's just cake and ice cream with the family and Eva," I said.

"It's your fifteenth birthday. Put on something nice," she said firmly.

What was up with her all the sudden? After she left, I changed into a pair of comfortable but cute jeans and braided my hair into a long plait. I found the slouchy sweater that Mom had given me for Christmas. It was pale pink, but it looked good with my complexion, despite the theory that redheads couldn't wear pink. I dabbed on a little lipstick and mascara and decided I was dressed up enough for a family celebration.

When I went downstairs, everyone had disappeared. "Ha, ha, very funny, you guys," I hollered, but the only sound I heard was the creak of a floorboard.

"Mom? Dad?" I was getting freaked out. The lights were off in the family room, but when I flipped on the switch, a chorus of voices shouted, "Surprise!"

The room was suddenly full of family and friends. Mom clapped her hands. "We did it!" she crowed. "We actually managed to surprise you. I thought for sure Katie was going to tell you. She was bursting to say something all week."

Eva gave me a hug. "Happy birthday, Jessica!"

"You knew about all this?"

"Yes," she said. "I helped your mom with the guest list."

"I see," I said. I'd spotted Connor and Dominic in the crowd, along with my fellow viragos Flo, Raven, and Andy. "It looks like you invited everyone in Nightshade."

"Almost," Eva said. "There were a few people who couldn't make it. But Flo has a surprise for you."

"Later," Flo said. She gave my best friend a warning look and Eva made an elaborate *lips are sealed* gesture.

There had to be at least fifty people in my house, including our next-door neighbors the Giordanos and the members of Side Effects May Vary. My sisters and Mom were standing in a little cluster by the French doors.

"Mom, this is amazing," I said.

"You didn't even have a clue, did you?" asked my sister Sydney.

I grinned at her. "I can't believe you didn't spill it."

"Jessica, go answer that, will you?" Mom said.

"How could you hear the door?" I asked her, but she just gave me a mom look. I did as she asked. My brother Sean was on the porch, holding hands with Sam.

I launched myself at him. "You came!"

"I wouldn't miss my little sister's birthday," he said. "You're only twelve once."

I punched him in the arm, hard. "Ha, ha, very funny."

"Hey, that hurt! You're getting strong."

"Samantha," I said, remembering my manners. "I'm so glad you could make it."

I grabbed their hands and dragged them into the family room. "Look who I found on our doorstep."

Mom and Dad and all my little sisters started talking at Sean at once. Katie hung on his arm while Sean did bicep curls.

My big brother caught us up with college life and then said, "Is there anything to eat? I'm starved."

While Dad fixed Sean a plate, I went over to talk to Samantha, who had made a beeline for her best friend and my next-door neighbor, Daisy Giordano.

"Hi, Daisy," I said. "Thanks for coming."

"Have you seen the cake yet?" Samantha asked. "Daisy made it."

"You did?" I asked. "Is it white cake with strawberries again?"

Samantha laughed at my gloomy tone.

"I convinced your mom to try something different this year," Daisy said.

I looked around, trying to be casual. "Where's Ryan tonight?"

"He's doing nightshift training for the police force," Daisy said succinctly. "But he sends his best wishes."

"Oh," I said. I tried not to let my disappointment show. Ryan Mendez was my brother's best friend, and I'd had a major crush on him for years. He and Daisy made a cute couple, but a tiny part of me would always have a thing for him.

A girl I didn't recognize approached me and tapped me on the shoulder. "Hi," she said. "I'm Stella. My older sister Sheila is your dad's accountant. He invited us to the party. Happy birthday, by the way."

"It's nice to meet you," I said. "Do you go to Nightshade High?" She looked about my age, but I hadn't seen her at school.

Stella shook her head. "Nope, we're from San Carlos." She fidgeted before she said, "I heard you play guitar."

"I do," I said. "Are you into music?"

"I'm in a band, actually," she said. "Me and my three sisters. We're called Wet Noodles for Three. We're playing at the Battle of the Bands."

"Cool!" I said. "I saw you play at the Black Opal once. You were great!" Wet Noodles for Three sounded like a sixties girl group, like the Ronettes or something.

As I laughed and talked to Stella, I watched Dominic out of the corner of my eye as he played a game of cards with my sisters Katie and Kellie. Flo walked over to him and said something. Katie and Kellie clapped their hands, and Dominic stood and walked through the French doors to the backyard patio. His Aunt Katrina and Flo's boyfriend Vinnie followed him a minute later.

Katie came over and tugged at Samantha's hand. "It's time for Jessica's surprise," she said importantly.

"Another surprise?"

Samantha shrugged. "Let's go investigate."

There was a stage set up in the backyard where the members of Side Effects May Vary were tuning up their instruments. The rest of the guests trickled in and took

50

seats on the lawn or in chairs scattered around. My sisters, Katie, Kellie, and Grace, were perched in the tree house that Dad had finally built them right before Christmas, while Fiona, Sydney, and Sarah grabbed prime front-row seats.

"This is the birthday girl's chair," Dad said. He had the camcorder in one hand as he waved to the easy chair he'd dragged out of the home office he and Mom shared.

I looked around for Eva, but she was in the back, holding hands with Evan. Connor was sitting at the patio table with Noel, Harmony, and Selena, but he caught me looking at him and we locked eyes until Selena said something to him and he finally looked away.

Teddie Myles stood at the back with a guy about her age, who was a little overdressed in a suit and tie. I assumed he was her date.

I went over to say hi and she introduced us. "Jessica, this is Mitch Peverell. He's looking for new talent during the Battle of the Bands."

I shook his hand. "So you're the agent everyone is talking about," I replied. "There's a lot of talent in Nightshade."

"Including Jessica," Teddie said. "She's an excellent guitar player."

How did she know that?

"Ms. Minerva is an old friend," Teddie explained.

"And she sang your praises. She has trained some of the best musicians in Nightshade," she said to Mr. Peverell.

Ms. Minerva thought I was a good guitar player? And she was friends with Teddie? I wasn't sure which piece of information surprised me more.

Mr. Peverell's eyes narrowed. "Tell me more about it. Are you in one of the bands competing?"

I laughed. "It's strictly a hobby," I said. "I'm too shy to get up there in front of people."

Side Effects May Vary took the makeshift stage and Dominic stepped up to the microphone.

"You're about to see the band to beat," I told Mr. Peverell. "Side Effects May Vary is the most popular act in Nightshade."

My attention turned to Dominic, and that's when I noticed that his eyes were rolling back into his head. He had that look, the one he got just before he broke into prophetic song.

I was right. I'd never heard them perform the song "Watch Your Step" by Elvis Costello. And Jeff Cool had a distinct look on his face, the one he got when Dominic went off the set-list, like he smelled something bad.

"Poor Dom," Raven whispered.

Poor Dom was right. His face was bone white and his hands kept clenching and unclenching, as if he were willing himself to sing the planned song. Despite his internal battle, the lyrics to "Watch Your Step" continued to stream from his mouth. Dominic always sounded good, even when he was throwing out a clue to whatever current mystery was happening in Nightshade. Unfortunately, I wasn't as good at figuring out the meaning behind the clues.

The song ended and Dominic regained his focus.

"Happy birthday, Jessica," he said. I thought he was going to launch into a birthday song, but instead the R.E.M. song "Drive" came out of his mouth. Was he having a premonition? I couldn't tell for sure. He was getting better at hiding it.

There was a loud round of applause after the song ended.

"See what I mean?" I asked Teddie and Mr. Peverell.

He stared at Dominic. "Yes, he's very talented." He didn't sound that happy about it.

I gave him a puzzled look, but before I could say anything, Mom, Dad, and Katie came out of the house. My parents carried an enormous chocolate cake. Katie led me to a table and pulled out a chair. I sat and then they placed it in front of me. Thick curls of chocolate covered the cake and I had to restrain myself from peeling off a piece.

"It's gorgeous," I said.

As Dad lit the candles, Dominic grabbed his guitar and said, "And now, please join us in singing 'Happy

Birthday' to Jessica." They sang and then I made a wish, one from my heart, and blew out the candles.

"Seriously, thank you all for celebrating my birthday with me," I said.

"Cut the cake!" Andy yelled. Everyone laughed.

But before I could, there was the strum of a guitar and then Dominic was singing again. The song was "For You" by Duncan Sheik. He walked to where I sat and stood in front of me a few feet away. It felt like there was no one else there. This time I knew he was singing to me and me alone.

I was a sucker for a boy with a guitar, especially this particular boy. When the song ended, I thought he'd say something, maybe even kiss me in front of all those people, but instead he turned and walked away.

I was still sitting there, stunned, when Eva came up and asked, "What do you make of that?"

"I have no idea," I said. "I wish he could make up his mind."

"Easier said than done," she murmured.

"That's not comforting," I told her.

"It's not meant to be," she said. But she gave my shoulder a squeeze as she said it.

The band exited after Dominic, then Connor ran up to the stage with a guitar in hand. "I'd like to sing something for Jessica's birthday," he said. He clipped on his guitar and said, "Check, check."

Connor dragged a chair to the stage and sat, fiddling with the straps of his guitar nervously. He took a deep breath and then strummed the first chord. The whole crowd went silent when he started to sing.

Selena and Harmony both pushed their way to the front. I struggled to identify the song Connor sang, but I couldn't place it. The emotion in his voice gave me chills, though. He looked right at me as he sang and I couldn't look away.

The song ended and everyone applauded, but Connor was still staring at me. I had to admit I kind of liked the attention.

"Didn't I tell you?" I overheard Teddie say to Mr. Peverell.

"You certainly didn't exaggerate the raw talent pool," he said.

My family helped me pass out slices of the cake. It had coconut filling and melt-in-your-mouth chocolate frosting. I handed two pieces to Daisy.

"The other one's for Ryan," I said, then blushed when she smiled at me.

"That's very considerate of you," she replied.

"Can I ask you something?" I couldn't look at her as I said it.

"Ask away."

"It's kind of personal," I said. "About you and Ryan."

"Go on," she said, but more cautiously.

"Were you two always in love?" I asked. "I mean — oh, that didn't come out right."

"I think I know what you're trying to say," she said gently. "And Ryan and I were friends for a long time before we became anything else. Sometimes, you need to be friends first."

I finally put my head up and saw that she was looking at Dominic. I couldn't believe I had just asked advice from a psychic. I wondered what thoughts of mine she'd picked up. "Thanks, Daisy."

"And Jessica," she said, "just give him some time, okay?"

"Okay." Her reply answered my question. She had picked up on something with her psychic powers, but it turned out it didn't bug me that Daisy knew exactly what I was feeling.

Dominic was sitting with Katie. My baby sister's hair was in wild curls around her face and there was a streak of frosting on her cheek, but she ate her cake contentedly next to him. He looked more at ease than he had all night.

I picked up his empty plate and a few others and took them inside. I was loading plates into the dishwasher when Dominic walked into the kitchen.

"I thought I might find you in here," he said.

"Here I am," I said. It was the first time we'd spoken all night.

"I wanted to give you your birthday present," he said.

"I thought the song was my present," I said. "Or was that a prediction?"

"Not a prediction," he replied. "Wishful thinking maybe."

"Does it have to be?" I asked. "Why can't we . . . I mean, in the fall you said you wanted to try . . ." I didn't know what else to say. He'd made it pretty clear that he didn't want to go out with me, at least not anymore.

"I did," he said. "I do. It's just that I can't."

I gulped. "I understand."

"Your arm is much better," he said.

My arm? For a second, I couldn't even remember what he was talking about, but then it came to me. That chupacabra bite had messed up my arm pretty good. I hadn't been able to play my guitar for several weeks afterwards.

Dominic had started to pull away almost as soon as the stitches were out.

He looked lost for a moment, then remembered why he had come to the kitchen. "Wait here."

He stepped out and came back with a large rectangular package.

I just stared at it. "You didn't have to."

"Open it," he coaxed. "I wanted you to see it when we were alone."

The package had been beautifully wrapped. I put a finger under one taped edge and tugged gently.

Inside was a case containing the purple Fender Stratocaster. I gasped and took it out carefully. "I thought Selena bought this," I said.

He laughed. "She wanted to, but I convinced her that another guitar there would match one of her other outfits better."

I couldn't take my eyes off the instrument. It was gorgeous and it was mine. "Dominic, it's too much. Thank you."

But when I looked up, he was gone.

CHAPTER SEVEN

I didn't have a chance to tell Eva about it until the next day.

"You mean he gave you an expensive guitar and then just left without saying anything else?" Eva asked.

I'd invited her to come over to my house to see the guitar, but really, I wanted my best friend's advice.

I nodded.

"He and Connor were giving each other dirty looks all night," Eva said. "And then that musical showdown."

"Musical showdown?"

"You have to realize that they were both singing about you," she said. "To you."

"I didn't recognize the song Connor sang," I admitted.

She snorted. "It was 'Fall for You.'" At my blank look, she added, "By Secondhand Serenade? No, nothing? Jessica, you really need to expand your playlist. That song is pretty romantic."

"Who has time?" I asked. "Romantic, huh?"

"Very," she said. "Now what are you going to do about it?"

"Nothing," I finally said. "I had my chance with Connor and I chose not to take it."

"Things change," she said. "He doesn't seem to be holding a grudge."

"It's complicated."

"That's what's great about it," she said.

"Only if you're on the outside looking in," I replied. "Otherwise, it's just confusing."

"We're teenagers. We're supposed to be confused," Eva said. "In the meantime, let's do something."

"What do you have in mind?"

She bounced up and down on the bed. "I don't know," she said. "Matinee?"

"There's nothing good out."

Eva's eyes lit up. "Want to go shopping?"

"That's a great idea. I got tons of gift cards for my birthday. But how are we going to get there?" I asked. It was doubtful Mom would have the time to take us.

"Bethany?" Eva suggested halfheartedly. Bethany was Eva's older sister.

"Nah," we said at once.

My phone rang. "What are you doing right now?"

Andy asked me. My fellow virago was always blunt and didn't always bother with greetings.

"Not much," I admitted. "Eva and I were talking about going to the mall."

"I'll pick you guys up in ten minutes," she said, and then hung up.

I stared at the phone. "We have a ride," I said. "I just need to ask Mom."

My mother was surprisingly agreeable, which I didn't get until she said, "Can you return these for me? Katie's feet have grown again and they don't fit her. I'm going to have to take her in, but I don't have time right now." Mom handed me a pair of shoes from Nordstrom and a receipt.

She kept a list of all our sizes and often bought something and made all the girls try it on until she found someone it fit, but Katie was the youngest. Hand-me-downs were completely worn out by the time they reached her, so she usually got something new.

"Do you need any money?"

"No, thanks."

Andy honked her horn and Eva and I dashed outside. She was in the driver's seat of an older Mercedes four-door. "New car?" I asked.

"Dad's," Andy said. "He hardly ever lets me drive it. But he's thinking about giving me his old one."

"Nice," I said. Sometimes I envied Andy being an only child. A little privacy once in a while might be a pleasant change.

"I'm glad you guys wanted to come," Andy replied. "Selena was busy."

I didn't spend too much friend time with Andy. She was intensely competitive and a total thrill-seeker. She'd also known forever that she was a virago, so she always acted like she knew more than everyone else.

And Selena Silvertongue was her best friend. Or at least she used to be.

"Everything okay?" I asked.

"Yeah," Andy said. "She's just been caught up with this new band she's in. They're playing today, you know. The first round of the Battle of the Bands is taking place right here at the mall."

My stomach did a little flip. I wondered if Dominic would be there too.

"Cool," Eva said. "But why are they playing at the mall?"

"It's good exposure for the merchants who are sponsoring the contest," Andy said. "Plus, the acoustics are great in there."

There were plenty of parking spots at the mall. Andy

found one right up front. We hit the food court for lemonades and then strolled along, window-shopping.

Andy seemed a little sulky after we spotted Selena in a store with Harmony.

"Do you want to say hi?" I asked.

"No," Andy said. "Let them have their band bonding or whatever. Besides, it looks like Selena's helping Harmony pick out new clothes. She's been losing weight lately so she probably needs some."

Now that Andy mentioned it, I did notice that Harmony had lost some weight. I wondered if her makeover had to do with the band or something else.

"Those two are practically attached at the hip these days," Eva said. "Remember when we saw them at the estate sale, Jess?"

"Estate sale?" Andy said. "What were they doing there?"

"Buying music stuff," Eva said. "Did you hear about the theft?"

"Theft?" Andy repeated. After Eva filled her in, Andy said, "Jessica, why didn't you tell me? We should be investigating."

I shrugged. "My tattoo didn't even get warm."

"Maybe it's having an off day," Andy suggested. "You know the whirlwinds aren't a hundred percent accurate."

"They're not?" I was surprised by the information.

"Don't get me wrong," Andy replied. "They help, but you can't always count on it."

"I'm sure it's nothing the viragos need to worry about," I said to her. "I told Flo all about it, and she didn't seem to be worried."

"Yeah, well, Flo's a little preoccupied these days," Andy said.

"What do you mean?"

"Haven't you noticed?" Andy shook her head and her blond curls bounced. "Flo's in love."

"With Vinnie?" Eva asked.

"Of course with Vinnie," I said.

"I wouldn't be surprised if she retired from virago duty soon," Andy said.

I stopped walking. "Flo wouldn't do that."

"She and Vinnie are talking about getting married," Andy pointed out.

"So?"

"So that changes things," Andy said.

"I don't believe it," I said. "Even if they do get married, Flo isn't going to retire."

"Believe it," Andy said. "It's going to happen. We should be ready for it."

My stomach hurt at the thought. I changed the subject. "Aren't those cute?" I pointed to a random pair of jeans in a store window.

Andy snorted. "Yeah, if you're into mom jeans."

"I think they're cute," I replied.

She thought I wasn't looking and mouthed "Denial" to Eva.

They were honestly hideous, but I wasn't going to back down and let her know she was right.

"I have a gift card to Nordstrom's," I said. "And I have to take these back. Let's go in here."

We returned the shoes with no problem, but I couldn't find anything I wanted to buy with my gift card. Maybe because Andy had a comment for every single thing I tried on.

Pink sweats: "Clashes with your hair." Long black skirt: "Makes you look washed out."

Purple mini: "Not with your legs, I wouldn't." The last one was just mean because I knew that my legs were a plus. In fact, they were the one thing I really liked about my body.

"Andy, Jessica has the best legs in the freshman class," Eva said angrily.

"Who says?" Andy asked derisively.

"The entire freshman class," Eva snapped. "Plus, she's gone out with two hot guys this year. How many have you dated?"

That shut Andy up. But I felt bad when I caught a miserable expression cross her face at the mention of hot guys. Did she have a crush on someone? And if so, who was it?

I changed the subject. "Is anybody else hungry? Let's get smoothies. My treat."

"Let me guess," Andy said. "You have a gift card."

"I certainly do." We all laughed and the tension lifted.

We took the escalator up to the food court, where we ran into Dominic, Raven, and their Aunt Katrina.

"I'm so glad you guys made it," Raven said.

"We're checking out the competition before we perform," Katrina explained. "We're the fourth band today."

On the second floor, near the food court, there were neat rows of folding chairs set up in front of a stage adorned with a NIGHTSHADE BATTLE OF THE BANDS banner.

"Let's sit in the back," Dominic said.

The seats gradually filled up. I waved to Rose Giordano and her boyfriend, Nicholas Bone, who were sitting with Nicholas's dad.

Ms. Johns took the stage and announced the judges. There was a polite smattering of applause. The Battle of the Bands would be judged by three celebrity judges: Flo's songwriter friend Hunter Verrat; Talulah Crank, who owned the indie label Cranky Kitten; and Teddie Myles, the owner of the Black Opal and a famous former rock star.

They were going to have to judge more than fifty bands over the course of the month. I didn't envy them.

"Why isn't Mitch Peverell one of the judges?" I asked idly while we waited for the first band to take the stage.

"He represents one of the bands," Dominic said. "It'd be a conflict of interest."

Ms. Johns announced the first band. "And now, give a round of applause for Hamlin!"

The band took the stage and started to tune up. I realized I'd seen the guitar player before, getting out of the town car at Mr. Lindquist's estate sale. Hamlin launched into a deafeningly loud song. I fought the urge to clasp my hands over my ears and we were in the last row.

The band played three songs, and then, thankfully, their set was over, and we stood up to leave. Ms. Johns came out again and announced another band, Moonlight and Magic, so we sat back down. I'd never heard of the band before, but I certainly recognized the members when they walked onstage: Connor, Harmony, and Selena.

Selena played drums, Connor played guitar, and Harmony sang. It was amazing how much she'd improved. It was like she was a completely different person. I was happy to hear enthusiastic applause for them.

Then Ms. Johns announced Drew Barrymore's Boyfriends. There was a roar of applause from the audience.

The Hamlin fans had sour looks on their faces as DBBF took the stage.

Scotty Turntable's performance was the hit of the show.

"He's got a ton of charisma," Raven commented. She wasn't kidding. Scotty was practically causing girls to faint. After their performance, DBBF were surrounded by squealing fans.

They announced a ten-minute break, and we stood up to stretch our legs. A couple of girls went up to Connor and asked him for his autograph. I noticed he spent a lot of time talking to a pretty brunette. I had to suppress a twinge of jealousy. What was wrong with me? I didn't know what I wanted. Or who.

Eva and I went over to say hi to Rose, who was Daisy's older sister.

"Hi, Rose," I said. "I haven't seen you around lately."

"So much homework," she said. "And I've been busy in the lab, too." Rose was a science major at UC Nightshade.

We joined a group of girls from school. Mitch Peverell, the talent agent, was talking to them. "Who is your favorite member of Drew Barrymore's Boyfriends?"

"I like Trevor," a tall brunette said.

"Not me," her friend, a blond girl with a purple streak

in her hair, said. "Scotty Turntable is the heart and soul of DBBF."

"And why is that?" Mr. Peverell asked intently.

"He writes all the songs," the blonde stated. "And he started the band."

Nicholas's dad, Mr. Bone, came up and shook Mr. Peverell's hand.

"Fine show," Mr. Bone pronounced. "I really enjoyed Hamlin." He wore his customary loud Hawaiian shirt and khaki shorts. "Fine show, indeed."

Eva gave me a look, but we both nodded politely. We said our goodbyes, but we were barely out of earshot when Eva said, "Maybe the fumes finally got to him."

"What do you mean?"

"I hear formaldehyde rots the brain," she replied darkly. Mr. Bone was the town undertaker.

Then I remembered that Rose was psychic, a telepath, which meant she'd probably read Eva's mind and heard what she'd said even before she said it aloud. And we were talking about her boyfriend's father.

"People have different tastes in music," I said.

Dominic, Raven, and their Aunt Katrina still sat in the back row. Katrina was staring at the now empty stage. "I'm going over to talk to him," she said. She twirled her hair when she talked.

When she came back, Katrina's eyes were strangely dilated. "Wasn't he just the best?" she breathed. "His name is Brett."

"You mean Scotty Turntable?" I asked. "I liked their new song, but the guitar player in Hamlin—"

"I know," she said. I thought she was agreeing how terrible he was, but her next words cleared that up. "Brett was the best thing about Hamlin."

Dominic stared at his aunt. "He was?"

She nodded fervently.

I had assumed she was talking about Drew Barrymore's Boyfriends. Eva and I exchanged puzzled looks behind her back. Hamlin's guitarist, Brett, could barely hold his guitar.

"You liked his playing, then?" Dominic asked carefully.

"Liked it?" she asked. "I didn't like it, I loved it! Look what I have!" She held out a Hamlin tee.

Katrina was a killer bass player. There was no way she could admire an amateur performance like that. But apparently she did. She lost interest in our conversation and gravitated back to Brett, who wore a Hamlin trucker hat and satin jacket.

Dominic finally had to drag her away so they could get ready for their set.

Side Effects May Vary were fabulous, as usual, but I noticed Mitch Peverell at the back, watching them with a frown on his face.

When Katrina took the stage, she wasn't wearing her naughty nurse's outfit or even her leopard print thigh-high boots and black micro mini. She wasn't even wearing a wig. Instead, she came out with her hair in pigtails and plain old jeans and a T-shirt.

"That's a new look for her," Eva commented.

"It's a Hamlin tee," I said. I pointed to the band's name in enormous letters on the front of her shirt.

"She's got it bad for that singer," Eva said.

"Katrina wouldn't change her entire look just to please some guy," I said firmly. "And besides, they just met."

Eva shrugged. "Stranger things have happened."

"I don't believe in love at first sight," I said. But as I looked at Dominic up on the stage, I couldn't help but remember how head over heels I had felt the first time I had heard him sing.

After the set ended and we were saying our goodbyes, Jeff Cool grabbed a skateboard from one of the kids in the crowd and hopped on it. He wobbled at first, but then whizzed past us through the food court, dodging frazzled diners.

"Jeff, quit clowning around," Dominic yelled, but Jeff ignored him.

He turned and then gathered speed as he headed for the escalator.

"I've never seen him on a board," Dominic said nervously. "I doubt he's ever skated in his life."

"He doesn't have a helmet or pads on," Raven commented. "If he falls, he's going to get hurt."

The skateboard clattered down a few steps of the escalator — but Jeff wasn't on it. We ran to the railing and watched in horror as he flew. As he landed in the fountain on the first floor, he put his arms out to catch himself. There was a loud snapping sound when he went down.

"Someone call an ambulance!" Katrina ordered.

"On it!" Rose said. She was talking to the dispatcher on her cell, but ran down the escalator steps.

We followed her. She bent down next to Jeff. "Hang on."

"Should we move him?" I asked. The water in the fountain had to be cold. Fortunately, someone from mall security turned off the water.

Paramedics arrived and tended to Jeff's injuries. It looked like both of his arms were broken.

"How did this happen?" Dominic said. "How are we going to perform without a guitarist?"

After they'd taken Jeff out in a gurney, the crowd dispersed.

"Let's go home," Andy said. "I've had enough excitement for one day."

Jeff was a showoff most of the time, but what had possessed him to hop on a skateboard?

CHAPTER EIGHT

There was no school on Monday because of a teachers' in-service day, which meant it was time to tackle cleaning the dollhouse. Katie and Kellie would be up and nagging me before too long. I carried the dollhouse castle into the backyard and tried not to make any noise. Everyone else in my family was still sleeping.

The outside of the castle was covered in a layer of dust. I took a damp rag and sponged it off. While I worked, I heard a squeaking noise, but when I looked around, I couldn't find anything to account for such an odd sound.

"I wish I could figure out what that sound was," I muttered. The sound grew louder until I realized it came from the inside of the dollhouse.

I opened it carefully and prayed that it wasn't a rat. Instead of a rodent, a doll stared up at me with wide, unblinking eyes. She wore a cornflower blue silk dress and a tiny crown upon her head. "Are you a simpleton?" she squeaked.

I stared at her slack-jawed.

"A peasant, then? You are quite as filthy as one," she said. Her delicate nose turned up as if she smelled something bad.

"Hey, no call for insults!" My long white T-shirt nightie and fuzzy socks were covered in dust and grime. "Have some manners, Blondie!" I couldn't believe I was arguing with a doll.

I dialed Eva's cell phone number and waited for her to answer. "You've got to get over here now," I said in a low voice. "You're not going to believe it! Come straight to my backyard." I wanted Eva there to reassure me that I hadn't let the attic dust get into my brain or something.

I peeked over at the princess. She ignored me as she sat down at a vanity in front of a gilt mirror, took off her crown, and brushed her long golden locks.

Her bedroom was all white and gold, with the bed in the shape of a swan. Another bedroom, painted azure blue, had an elaborately carved bed and a bearskin rug on the floor. It looked masculine, but I didn't see a prince anywhere.

Eva rushed into my backyard about fifteen minutes later. Her face was red from running. "What could possibly be so important that I had to tear over here at" — she stopped to catch her breath — "eight o'clock in the morning?"

"This," I said.

I pointed to the dollhouse.

"You want to play dolls?" she asked. The look of confusion on her face made me laugh.

"No," I said. "Check this out." The princess doll continued to brush her hair with her tiny gold brush.

"That's . . . that's . . . amazing!" she replied.

We stared at the dollhouse. A suit of armor walked down the great stone hall. A black mastiff followed behind him.

In the kitchen, a rosy-cheeked cook opened the door of a copper stove and put in a pie.

Eva produced her handheld camcorder from the pocket of her hoodie. "I've got to shoot this," she said.

The princess barked out an order and the tiny figures froze. No matter how much Eva tried coaxing them, the castle occupants would not move.

"Stop motion will work," Eva said. She picked up the princess and placed her in her swan bed. A sulky expression crossed the princess's face. Eva muttered to herself as she put the other dolls in various poses.

"What's your name, anyway?" I asked the doll.

"Shoot," Eva said. "I'm almost out of memory. I can't wait until I can afford a decent camcorder."

As soon as Eva stopped recording, the princess spoke.

"I am Princess Antonia," she said. "But you may call me Your Royal Highness."

I decided to try killing her with kindness. "How may I be of assistance, Your Highness?"

"My prince is missing," she said. "We are supposed to live happily ever after, and how are we to do that when I cannot even find him?"

I couldn't manage my own love life. I wasn't sure I could help a six-inch animated doll find true happiness.

"Maybe he's still in Natalie's attic," Eva commented.

Princess Antonia smothered a sob. "I am bereft without him."

Eva and I exchanged a glance. The princess was a little over the top. "When did you see him last?" I finally asked. I didn't really have time to look for her pint-sized prince, but I still felt sorry for her.

Princess Antonia wore the smile of someone who was used to getting her own way. "Yesterday," she said. "He has been looking upon my pleasing visage for an eternity. Your wish craft allowed him to move about the castle."

"Wish craft?" I asked.

"You do not even know the kind of magic you have wrought?" she said scornfully. "The powder is very powerful. A beginning sorceress should not attempt to use it."

"And then what happened to the prince?"

"He made his bows and pledged his love and then simply vanished," she said.

Where could someone hide in a dollhouse? Then I realized that, because of the wishing powder, he could have simply opened the door and left.

"There's no way Natalie knew about this," Eva said. "It's a magical dollhouse."

"I don't know," I replied. "This didn't happen until I spilled some of that indigo powder in there. What should I do?"

"Call Natalie," Eva suggested. "She's a witch, right? She should be able to help."

I tried her number, but it went straight to voice mail.

A moment later, two miniature knights began to battle in the garden.

I tried Natalie's number again, but there was no answer. "It's no use," I said. "I'm going to have to call Selena."

Selena was the only other witch I knew and I was desperate.

When I called her and told her I needed help, she said, "This better be good," and then hung up on me.

Selena looked unbelievably good for early morning. Her blond hair was perfectly flat-ironed, and she wore denim jeans and a jade top with a matching jade necklace.

"What is it?" she asked.

Eva and I pointed to the dollhouse.

Selena peeked into the princess's bedroom, and the little doll screamed, "Sorceress!"

"How did this happen?" she asked.

"I don't know," I said. Denial was the best option.

Selena continued to question us. "Where did you get the dollhouse?"

"In Natalie's attic," Eva said.

She ran a finger along the floor of the ballroom and it came back stained blue.

She held it to her nose and sniffed. "Wishing powder," she said. "Very rare. I don't suppose you know anything about that, either?"

"Wishing power?" Eva said. "You mean I could sprinkle some of that stuff and wish for anything I wanted?"

"Pretty much," she said. "But as with any magic, the wish may come with a price. This stuff can be dangerous."

"I wish —" Eva started to say, but Selena and I both yelled "No!" at the same time.

"It's worth a small fortune," Selena said. "Do you have any more of it?"

I didn't answer her question. I wanted to give the wishing powder back to Natalie and be done with it as soon as Selena reversed the spell.

"The dollhouse was like this when I woke up this morning," I said. It was true.

"I'm going to have to do some research," she said.

"Another amateur!" the princess shrieked.

Selena rolled her eyes. "I'll call you if I find out anything."

As she started to walk away, I had second thoughts. "Actually," I said, "I don't think we'll need you to reverse the spell after all, Selena." The princess had warned that it wasn't a job for a beginner, and I didn't want to mess anything up worse than it already was.

"Are you serious?" Selena said. "Thanks for getting me out of bed early on a day off from school."

"I'm sorry," I said. "You can't tell anyone. Not even your aunt."

"I promise," she replied before storming away. I imagined that Selena's aunt, sorceress Circe Silvertongue, would love to get her hands on wishing powder, but she wasn't the only one. Hunter wanted something badly enough to break into the Mason house. Had he been looking for the wishing powder?

Although I'd gotten used to Flo's grueling training sessions, I also liked to run on my own. After Eva left, I went for a run to clear my head. I put on my headphones and turned my MP3 player to my favorite running playlist. Nobody but me had to know there were several Side Effects May Vary songs on it.

The Hamlin followers had set up camps all over the park, but my favorite route took me away from the most crowded sections.

My mind drifted as the miles went by. I ended my run, did a quick cooldown, and then lay under an oak tree and gulped down a bottle of water.

"Your mom thought I might find you here," Dominic said.

"Here I am." I was hot and sweaty, and he looked immaculate in a formfitting blue T-shirt that matched his eyes and faded blue jeans.

I waited for him to say something else, but he just stood there. Finally, I said, "I didn't think singers got up this early."

He acknowledged my weak joke with a polite smile. "I wanted to talk to you without anyone else around."

My heart gave a thud, but I steadied my breathing. "What's up?"

"My Aunt Katrina has been acting strange. She's been seeing that guy Brett."

I nodded. "Maybe she's in love."

"Brett is a complete doofus," Dominic replied. "He calls me 'sport.'"

"At least it's not 'buddy.'"

Dominic laughed, a real laugh this time. "You heard

his songs, though. All of this really whiny stuff about the father who abandoned him. It seems like he's fishing for sympathy."

Since Dominic's mom had abandoned him and Raven, I wondered if those songs hit too close to home. "Lyrics aside, Hamlin's music is just really bad," I said. "Your aunt usually has really good taste in music. I'm surprised she'd be so into them."

"Do you think it's strange that she likes him?"

I hesitated. "There's someone for everyone," I said. "But I had a weird feeling about the whole day at the mall."

"Did your tattoo warn you?" he asked.

"My tattoo hasn't budged lately," I said. Dominic's mom and sister were both viragos, so I didn't feel like I was spilling any trade secrets.

It was nice to have someone to talk to about it, but I was boring him. He stared off into space for so long that I finally cleared my throat.

"That doesn't mean there's not something going on," I pointed out.

"I'm worried," he admitted. "Last night at practice, I sang 'Masquerade.' That's a Backstreet Boys song." The disbelief in his voice made me giggle, but I stopped quickly when I saw his expression.

"That's not in your usual set list," I said.

"Do you think it's a clue?"

"It could be," I said cautiously. The thought of spending time crime-solving with him kind of freaked me out. "What does Raven think?"

"I haven't talked to her about it yet. You're the first person I've told."

I changed the subject. "What are you guys going to do about finding a replacement for Jeff?"

"I don't know," he said. "My Aunt Katrina knows this guy, but he's on tour until next month."

Dominic obviously just wanted to be friends and I wanted — well, I couldn't have what I wanted. The wisest thing seemed to be to avoid him, but I couldn't ignore it if Katrina was walking into danger, either.

"What does Raven think about what's going on with your aunt?"

"She thinks it's just a crush," Dominic said. "But I'm worried. Aunt Katrina's husband died a few years ago and she hasn't dated much since."

"You don't want to see her get hurt," I said.

He nodded.

"But you can't stop that," I told him. "Someone always gets hurt."

As if to illustrate my point, Brett Piper chose that

moment to arrive at the park with a woman on each arm. Women who were not Katrina. A roadie followed behind Brett, carrying his guitar.

Dominic's gaze followed mine. "I can't believe it. That worm."

I put a hand on his arm. "Wait and see what happens."

"Welcome, disciples of Hamlin," Brett said. All the Hamlin fans stopped whatever they were doing and surrounded him.

"Oh, brother," Dominic said, but I shushed him.

Brett walked among the people like he was some kind of god.

"Sing for us, Brett," someone said.

"Dear god no," I whispered. Dominic choked back a laugh.

"I do happen to have my guitar with me," Brett said.

Of course he did.

He snapped his fingers. "Hal, my guitar please." A roadie handed him the instrument.

"I don't think I can take another Brett performance," Dominic said.

Brett glanced our way and Dominic and I ducked behind a large oak tree. We huddled together. Our hands touched and neither of us moved away.

I cleared my throat. "Do you think he saw us?" I asked in a whisper.

"I don't know," Dominic replied. "But why are we hiding?"

"I'm not sure," I admitted. "But I have a feeling something is up." My tattoo had given a halfhearted little whirl and then stopped.

But I figured it out a little while later when Brett's performance ended and an older guy in an immaculate suit walked up to him. What was Mitch Peverell doing here?

I moved closer to hear what they were saying.

"Are you sure this is worth it?" Brett asked.

"Of course it's worth it," Mr. Peverell said. "Look around you. They love you. You're a star. And it's my job to make sure you stay in the spotlight. Whatever it takes."

What exactly was Mr. Peverell willing to do for his client?

CHAPTER NINE

Friday night, Eva and I went to see more bands perform. The weather had cooperated and the park had been transformed into a concert venue, complete with food and drink kiosks.

Eva and I stopped at a booth selling T-shirts. She bought a Battle of the Bands tee and I opted for a Wet Noodles for Three tee.

Dominic and Raven were already there, sitting at a table near the stage with some of the band. Katrina was with Brett Piper at a table for two.

"Wanna go hang out with Raven?" Eva asked.

"Sure," I replied. "Raven's our friend. Just because my relationship with her brother didn't work out doesn't mean we should avoid her." As much as I wanted to stay away from Dominic until my sore heart healed, it didn't look like it was going to happen.

I thought sitting opposite Dominic would keep some

distance between us, but instead, we were forced to look at each other.

Dominic and the rest of the band were freaking out at the news that Jeff Cool would be out for at least six weeks. They were going to have to find someone to replace him and fast. They'd already performed in the first round of Battle of the Bands and received a top score, which was good news.

As the band members hashed it out, a familiar girl approached the table.

"Hi, Stella," I said. "I wondered if I'd see you here."

"Hi, Jessica," she said. "I like your T-shirt." She gestured at my new purchase.

"Thanks," I said. "Is your band playing tonight?"

"No," she said. "There's been an accident. Didn't you hear?"

"Hear what?" Raven asked anxiously.

Stella sighed. "Our guitarist, my sister Sheila, had to have like a hundred stitches."

"What happened?" Dominic asked.

"She was juggling knives and dropped them," Stella said.

"Why was she juggling knives?" Eva asked.

"Good question," Stella answered. "Supposedly, Sheila doesn't even remember why she did it." She looked at her watch. "I better get home to help her change the bandages." She wished the members of Side Effects May Vary good luck and left the park.

"Pretty stupid thing to do right before the Battle of the Bands," Raven said. "Especially since she'd never done anything like it before."

First Jeff and now Sheila. Was it just bad luck or something more sinister? It was Nightshade, so I was going to go with sinister.

Eva nudged me. "I do love a man in uniform."

I looked over. Ryan Mendez stood there in a police officer's uniform. I kept looking. He did wear it well.

"I didn't think he was through with his training yet," I said.

"He's not," Dominic said. "That's a Guardian uniform."

"What's a Guardian?"

He laughed. "Worried they're horning in on virago territory? Don't be. The Nightshade Guardians is a volunteer program for people in their late teens and early twenties who are interested in law enforcement. The new chief started it."

The Battle of the Bands got under way, and we turned our attention to the stage. The first two bands weren't very impressive. I was pretty sure they wouldn't advance to the next round. People in the audience started to drift away, but then Magic and Moonlight took the stage.

"I didn't know Connor's band was playing," I said.

"You didn't?" Dominic said in a suddenly snarky tone. "I thought that's why you were here."

He sounded jealous. His sister gave him a look and then said, "Jessica can date anybody she wants, remember?"

I was relieved when the music started. Connor did sound good, and he was getting more comfortable onstage. In fact, he had his own group of admirers, who stood next to the stage and screamed his name every other second.

After the set ended, I said, "I could use a soda. Anybody want anything?"

"I'll go with you," Dominic said.

We were in line when I spotted Mitch Peverell handing out Hamlin buttons. Dominic nudged me. "Want me to get you one?"

"I prefer Side Effects May Vary, thanks," I said.

A girl in front of us heard me and turned around. "Me too!" she squealed. She didn't seem to recognize the lead singer standing next to me, but Dominic's hair was covered by a beanie and he wore sunglasses.

Mr. Peverell came over and handed her a button. "Have you heard Hamlin?" he asked.

She sent me a panicked look, but nodded to him politely. "Yes."

"What do you like about the other band?" he asked. "Jeff Cool?"

"N-not really," she stuttered.

"But I was told that Jeff wrote all the songs for Side Effects May Vary," Mr. Peverell persisted. "And that he's the leader of the group."

Dominic snorted, but didn't comment.

"Side Effects May Vary plays covers," I said. "And Jeff isn't the leader of the group. Katrina Phillips is."

"Hmm," Mr. Peverell replied. "Good to know."

"And all the girls go to see the lead singer, Dominic Gray," the girl in front of us said.

"Interesting." Mr. Peverell handed me a button. "Here, take one," he said, before he hurried off to catch his next victim.

I waited until he was out of sight before pitching it right into the recycling bin. "What is with that guy?"

"He's pretty intense," Dominic said. "But he's good at what he does. Hamlin was completely unknown until he signed them. Now everyone says they're the next big thing. If they win the Battle of the Bands, there will be no stopping them."

"That's a scary thought," I replied. We walked back to the table in silence, but I couldn't help thinking that there was a lot at stake for the musicians in Nightshade right now.

CHAPTER TEN

The Battle continued over the next week, but I had other things on my mind. Like that I hadn't practiced enough. I decided to take the guitar Dominic had given me to my lesson. Ms. Minerva didn't answer the first or second time I rang the doorbell. She scheduled exactly five minutes between lessons. I checked my watch. I was on time, which was a relief. If I wasn't, she'd boot me out in a second. Ms. Minerva had no tolerance for tardiness.

I couldn't hear anyone else playing, and the house was silent and dark. It was almost unheard of, but my normally punctual guitar teacher appeared to be running late. I sat in a chair on her front porch and waited. It was an uncomfortable wooden chair with a high straight back. Ms. Minerva probably didn't want to encourage lounging around.

I waited about ten minutes, but there was no sign of

her. I was worried that something had happened to her. I rang the doorbell again and finally pounded on the door.

Then I remembered that Connor's lesson was usually right before mine. I pulled out my cell and called him. He answered on the first ring.

"Jessica, I was just getting ready to call you."

"I'm at Ms. Minerva's, but she's not answering."

"That's what I was going to call you about. I hung around for half an hour, but she never showed."

"That's not like her," I said.

"I know," he said. "Maybe we should call someone."

My whirlwind tattoo began to tingle. Something was wrong.

"Connor, I'll call you back." I hung up the phone and ran to the backyard. I peered through the sliding glass door into her living room. The room was filled with smoke and Ms. Minerva was stretched out on the couch, not moving. She could die if I didn't do something.

The door was cool to the touch and unlocked. I opened it and squeezed through. Much of the smoke escaped through the open door, but I couldn't see any obvious source of fire.

I checked for a pulse and was relieved to find she was breathing.

Finally, I realized the smoke came from the stove

in the kitchen. I turned off the oven and cracked all the windows.

I spotted a fish tank by a kitchen window and gasped. I hoped her fish hadn't died from the smoke. I looked in and was glad to see the fish still swimming around. There was something floating in the water and I scooped it out with a net.

It was a guitar pick. I dried it off on my shirt and put it in my pocket. I went back to check on Ms. Minerva. This time, she stirred when I touched her and then sat up. "Jessica, what are you doing here?" She yawned and stretched.

"Are you okay?" I asked.

"Just a little tired," she said. "I must have dozed off. I was baking brownies for that nice young man."

"What nice young man?" I asked, but she ignored the question.

"How did you get inside?" Her gaze sharpened with suspicion.

"I had a lesson at four," I said. "You didn't answer the door, so I came around back and saw you lying there."

She put a hand to her head. "I was having such a nice chat," she said. "He played for me. Quite well, in fact, but I didn't recognize the music. I decided to bake brownies, but then I fell asleep."

"Someone was playing here?" I asked. "One of your students?"

A look of confusion crossed her face. "I don't remember."

I hesitated. "Is there someone I can call to stay with you?"

We were interrupted by pounding on the door. "Ms. Minerva, it's Chief Wells. Are you all right?"

"Jessica, could you please answer that for me?" Ms. Minerva asked. "I still feel a little woozy."

I opened the door as Chief Wells prepared to pound on the door again, and she lurched forward a bit.

"Wait, I know you," she said. "You show up at an awful lot of crime scenes."

"So do you," I said, joking, but she frowned. I held out a hand. "Jessica Walsh."

"Well, Jessica Walsh, what exactly are you doing here?"

I opened the door wide. "Come on in, Chief Wells. This is my guitar teacher's house."

"Guitar, huh?" she said. "That explains a lot."

The chief strode into the living room and introduced herself to Ms. Minerva. "One of your neighbors reported a suspicious character in your backyard. She thought someone broke into your house."

"That was Jessica," Ms. Minerva said, obviously not aware of how it would sound to the chief.

"Ms. Minerva didn't answer the door at our scheduled time, so I came around to the back and saw her lying on the couch."

"So you broke in," Chief Wells said. It wasn't a question.

"The back door was open," I explained carefully. "There was smoke all over the place. And I was worried about my teacher."

"But I'm fine. I had just dozed off," Ms. Minerva said.

"I don't see any smoke," Chief Wells said. "How did the fire happen?"

"I don't know," Ms. Minerva said. "I'll check." I helped her to her feet.

"There was something burning in the oven," I said. "I turned the oven off and opened all the windows to clear the smoke."

The chief asked Ms. Minerva, "Where do you keep your valuables?"

"I don't really have any valuables," Ms. Minerva replied. "Except — oh, no!" She rushed to a cabinet and drew out a violin case. "My grandfather's violin," she said. She opened the case slowly, as if afraid of what she'd find. "It's here."

"Anything else of value to a thief?" Chief Wells prodded.

She shook her head. "Not unless it was something small."

"Why were you here again?" The chief was definitely unimpressed with me.

I gritted my teeth. "I had a lesson."

The chief went to the kitchen and returned a minute later. "Burnt brownies," she said. "But that doesn't mean you're telling the truth about everything else. Jessica, I'll have to ask you to check your backpack."

"What?" I was fuming mad, but I dumped out the contents of my bag and turned my pockets inside out. "There, are you satisfied?" My mind raced as the chief went through my backpack with an insulting thoroughness. She was just doing her job, but it was annoying how she believed the worst of me.

"One more thing," the chief said. She opened my guitar case and turned over my gorgeous purple guitar to see if there was anything hidden beneath it.

"Be careful with that," I said. I was working hard to control my anger.

"Jessica would never steal anything," Ms. Minerva protested. She swayed, and I grabbed her to help steady her. I led her back to the couch.

"She said there was someone here earlier," I said.

The chief looked skeptical. "Is that true, Ms. Minerva?"

"I don't remember. I'm not as young as I used to be," she said.

"Maybe we should get you to the doctor," the chief said gently, then turned to me. "Jessica, I suggest you go home. I may have a few more questions for you."

I halfway expected her to add something about not leaving town, but she simply turned her attention back to Ms. Minerva.

When I got outside, Connor was running up the street. "Jessica, is everything okay?"

I nodded and told him what had happened. "But Chief Wells has it under control now."

Just then, the Slim's Diner van careened around the corner. As expected, Flo was behind the wheel, with Andy and Raven in the back. Their tattoos must have alerted them to the danger too.

"What's going on?" Flo asked.

Connor and I exchanged a look. I decided that if I couldn't trust my trainer, who could I trust?

"Our guitar teacher almost set her house on fire," I said. "But, um, the chief of police is in there now, so . . ."

"Why didn't you call me?" Flo snapped. Today's tee read BECAUSE I SAID SO, THAT'S WHY.

Of course I should have told her. "I'm sorry, Flo," I replied. "I wasn't thinking."

Connor's mouth dropped open, but he rallied quickly. "Why should Jessica have called you?" he asked her curiously.

I waited to see what Flo would say, but she didn't respond for a long moment. She couldn't exactly announce that she was my trainer, my mentor, my *boss*.

"Because I have a key to her house," she finally said. "I feed her cat while she's on vacation."

"I didn't know Ms. Minerva had a cat," Connor said.

I cleared my throat. "I think you mean her fish," I said. I could hear Andy snickering in the back of the van.

Connor looked hurt, but he didn't argue. "Jessica, can I walk you home?"

I looked at Flo imploringly and she gave a tiny nod.

"Flo can give us both a ride home," I told him.

As predicted, Flo dropped off Connor first. He climbed out of her van, shoulders slumped, and said a halfhearted good night.

"He's cute," she said, after he was out of earshot.

"He is cute," I agreed.

"Cute, but not Dominic," Flo said. There wasn't a hint of sympathy in her voice.

"Nope."

"Hey, great save with that line about feeding her fish," Andy said. "Does Ms. Minerva even have a fish?"

"As a matter of fact, she does," I said. "And I found this in the tank." I produced the pick from my pocket.

"What is it?" Raven asked.

"It's a guitar pick," I said.

"She is a guitar teacher," Andy pointed out, rather unnecessarily, since I was her student.

"But what was it doing in her fish tank?" I asked, which shut Andy up.

"It's a custom-made pick," Flo said, glancing over at it as she drove.

Raven craned her neck for a better look. "It has DBBF on it."

"What's it mean?" Andy said, peering over my shoulder.

"It means that we need to talk to the members of Drew Barrymore's Boyfriends."

I still hadn't figured out what to do about the dollhouse, but I figured as long as I had Flo's attention, I could get her to help me.

After Flo had dropped off Raven and Andy, I said, "I have something to show you at my house, if you have a minute."

"Can it wait?" she asked. "I have to get back to the diner." Then she took a good look at the expression on my face. "Okay. I'm sure Daisy can cover for a little while longer."

"Where's Slim?" I asked.

"He surprised Natalie with a little getaway," she said.

"No wonder she isn't answering her phone," I replied. "I tried calling her about this first, since it's more her area of expertise."

"What is?" Flo asked as she parked the van on the street in front of my house.

"Let me show you," I said. My sisters had been asking about the dollhouse almost hourly, and I could tell it was getting on Mom's nerves. So, that morning I had finally given in and hauled it to their room. But first I had scooped up the seven lively occupants and put them in a shoebox with some holes poked in the top. Dismissing their protests, I closed the lid and then tied a piece of string around it. I wasn't sure what to do with it after that.

I took Flo up to my room and removed the box from under the bed. I opened it and the princess bounded to her feet and shook her tiny fist at me. "Blackguard! Cretin! I'll see you hanged for this."

I shut the lid, which muffled her shriek of rage.

"I think it happened because of wishing powder," I

said. "That's why I was trying to get in touch with Natalie. What should I do?"

She sighed. "Where's the powder?"

"In the closet," I said.

But when we checked my soccer bag, the wishing powder was gone.

"Who would want to take it?" Flo asked.

I hesitated. "What about Hunter?" I asked. "His hands were stained blue when he was in the attic."

"Hunter wouldn't steal a thing," she said.

"But I . . ." I looked at her expression and realized she wouldn't believe me.

"It's not him," she said sharply. "I'm sure of it. Did you tell anyone?"

I was afraid she was going to ask me that. "Selena."

"You told Selena Silvertongue that you had a box full of wishing powder?" Flo asked. "What were you thinking?"

"Selena wouldn't take it," I said. But I wasn't really that sure. She'd done some pretty questionable things in the past.

Just then, Mom appeared in the doorway of my room. "Jessica, what is the meaning of this?"

She held up the porcelain box, which used to contain the indigo powder. "I wish you'd tell me what this is. I was looking for Sarah's sweater in your closet and it fell out."

Mom's hands had a little residual blue powder on them.

"It's wishing powder," I blurted out involuntarily.

Flo shot me a dirty look. "It's mine," Flo said. "A temporary hair dye. The brand is Wishing Powder."

"Oh, you can't imagine what I was thinking," Mom said. She approved of Flo, so she handed over the box and wandered back into her office without another word.

"I couldn't help it," I said to Flo. "It's *wishing* powder. She made a wish. I had to tell her."

"That was a close call," she replied. "We'll have to wash this box out thoroughly so there are no more wishes granted. And I'll take this, too." She clutched the shoebox.

"But the powder that was in there is still gone," I said, frowning.

I couldn't convince Flo that it wasn't Selena. There was no way Flo would ever believe that her friend Hunter would steal anything. I was going to have to prove it.

CHAPTER ELEVEN

"We're all going to the Black Opal tonight," Flo announced on Saturday after training.

"I'll have to pass," I said.

"That wasn't an invitation," Flo said. "Battle of the Bands is tonight. And DBBF are playing."

"Who else is playing?" I asked, but I already knew the answer. I couldn't avoid Dominic no matter how hard I tried.

But Flo surprised me. "As of right now, nobody," she said. "Vinnie said they're trying to get a replacement for Jeff."

"Jessica plays the guitar," Andy reminded her.

"That's right," Flo said. "I have an idea. Jessica's going undercover. She's going to join Side Effects May Vary, temporarily, of course, and help us get to the bottom of this."

"No, I can't!" I couldn't think of anything more humiliating. Dominic would hate having me in the band and I would hate being there. Watching all those girls drooling over him would be pure torture.

"Why not?" Flo gave me a hard stare and I knew I'd better come up with a good excuse.

"My mom is already freaking out about how much I'm gone," I said. "I can't add anything else."

"I'll excuse you from training," Flo replied.

"It's not just that," I said. "I've never performed in front of a large crowd before."

"Don't worry," Raven said. "I'll talk to Dominic. He'll help you through it."

Flo was already dialing the phone. "Vinnie, I found someone to replace Jeff."

She stepped away from us to continue the conversation in private. She was smiling when she came back. "You're in."

"That's . . . great," I said weakly.

"They're going to try to squeeze in a practice this afternoon," Flo said. "Be at the Black Opal at three."

There was no sense in fighting the inevitable. I couldn't shirk my duty as a virago.

I got to the Black Opal at exactly three, but I was the first one there. Teddie Myles was sitting at one of the tables near the stage.

"Jessica, come sit with me," she said.

"If I'm not disturbing you," I said. Teddie had been a famous rock 'n' roll guitarist in the late sixties. She was Dominic's idol.

"I hear you joined a band," she said. "Sit down and tell me all about it."

"It's only temporary," I replied. I took a seat across from her.

She gave a snort of laughter. "That's what I said too. Spent thirty years in the business."

"It must have been amazing," I said.

Dominic walked in and frowned when he saw me sitting there. I guess that answered my question about how he felt about me joining the band.

"You're early," he said.

"I'm on time," I replied. "There's a difference."

Teddie got up from the table. "Jessica, it's been lovely talking to you, but there's some paperwork calling my name."

"You two seem friendly," Dominic said.

"I like her," I said. "Is that a problem?"

"Not a problem at all," he said. He took a seat opposite me. "Look, I wanted to talk to you before the rest of the band got here."

"About?"

"You don't have to join if you don't want to," he said.

"I know that." As much as Flo made it seem like an order, I knew I had a choice. But what I really thought he was saying was that *he* didn't want me in the band.

"It won't be hard for you because of us?" he asked.

"I'll manage to keep my hands off you," I replied sarcastically.

He blushed. "I didn't mean it like that." He moved in so close that our knees touched. "Besides, did you ever think that maybe I wouldn't be able to keep my hands off you?"

Now it was my turn to blush. "It makes it hard to think of you as a friend when you flirt with me like that."

"Maybe I don't want you to think of me as a friend," he replied. He leaned in even closer and I thought he was going to kiss me.

I scooted away, but my heart rate accelerated. "Then maybe you shouldn't have stopped dating me."

"Sorry we're late," Katrina said.

The rest of the band arrived and I stood. "Time for practice," I said.

"Can we talk later?" Dominic asked.

I nodded and then walked over to tune my purple guitar.

"Jessica, we're doing a short set tonight," Katrina said.

"Here's our set list. Do you know any of these songs?"

"I know that Buddy Holly song," I said. Ms. Minerva made sure that we learned a bunch of different kinds of music.

"Good," Katrina replied. "Then we'll work on teaching you the other two."

"What about 'Touch and Go'?" Vinnie suggested. "It's an old Cars song. There's a lot of drums, not as much guitar."

"Perfect," she said. "Let's get started."

We practiced for hours, but I still didn't have the song down. Even though they didn't say anything, I could tell the rest of the band was getting frustrated.

Teddie sat at one of the tables and watched us. Finally, she walked up to Dominic, who cut off in the middle of a song.

She said something too low for me to hear, and Dominic broke into a wide smile.

"Teddie has a great idea," he said.

"Jessica and Dominic, you should do 'Stop Draggin' My Heart Around' as a duet," she said. "An acoustic version." She brought out an acoustic guitar for me to borrow.

She didn't wait for a response, but went into her office in the back.

After she left, everybody started talking at once. "No," I said. "I can't sing."

"Of course you can sing," Dominic said. "You're in chorus."

"Yeah," I said. "But have you ever seen me try out for a solo? There's a reason for that."

"Dominic, don't pressure her," Katrina said. "If Jessica doesn't want to sing, we can think of something else."

The disappointment in her voice decided it for me. "I'll try," I said.

I strummed the first notes of the song and then tried not to look at Dominic as we sang, but it was difficult. The song was practically the anthem of our relationship so far.

We practiced right up until curtain time. The band voted and decided to start our set with the duet. I tried breathing exercises and singing scales while we were backstage waiting to go on, but the lump in my stomach wouldn't go away.

"You look like you're going to hurl," Katrina said, but gently. "Is this the first time you've ever sung in public?"

I nodded. "Unless you count in chorus, but there I'm singing with about fifty other people."

"Then pretend you're in chorus," she said with a shrug.

It was better than picturing the audience naked.

When we finally took our places on the stage, Dominic said, "I'd like to introduce our new band member, Jessica Walsh." He nodded at me and I strummed the first chord.

The duet with Dominic was intense. He held my eyes with his own as we sang. I couldn't look away. I didn't need to pretend. Everyone else in the room receded until it was just the two of us.

The spell was broken when the last note sounded, and the audience burst into loud cheers, then jumped to their feet. A standing ovation.

Dominic waited until the noise died down and then I went into the intro of the Buddy Holly song. But instead, Dominic sang "Stairway to Heaven."

The rest of the band figured out what was happening and changed songs, but I was slow to recognize it. There were a few embarrassing chords until I caught up.

The rest of the set went without a hitch, but Dominic was stony-faced as he sang. As soon as the last song was over, he stalked off the stage.

I followed him. "Was that a prophetic song?"

He ignored me and walked over to the opposite side of the room, where he was approached by his throng of admirers. I didn't follow him.

As I left the stage, I was shocked to see Chief Wells in the front row. Teddie Myles sat next to her. She waved at me to come over. I went reluctantly.

"Jessica, I wanted to introduce you to my little sister."

I looked around, but didn't see anyone besides the chief.

Teddie let out a bellow of laughter. "I get that a lot," she said. "This is my sister, Chief Louella Wells."

"We've met," the chief said shortly.

"The chief thinks I'm trouble," I explained to Teddie, only half-kidding.

She chuckled, but the chief didn't even crack a smile. Teddie turned to her sister and said, "You're barking up the wrong tree, Lou. Jessica is *special*." I wasn't imagining the emphasis she placed upon the word.

"Special? Like you were?" Chief Wells seemed skeptical until Teddie nodded gravely.

"Exactly like me."

"Interesting." The chief turned her gaze upon me and I squirmed.

"I'd better be going," I said. I was still having trouble accepting that the two of them were sisters.

Drew Barrymore's Boyfriends were up next, and while they played well enough to make it to the next round of the tournament, I couldn't help but notice the absence of their star, Scotty Turntable.

I caught up with DBBF's singer after their set. "Hi, there," I said.

"No autographs right now," he said.

"Oh, I'm not a fan," I said.

He gave me an offended look and I realized what I had said.

"No, I mean, I am a fan," I said. "But that's not why I want to talk to you."

"Go on," he said.

"I'm sorry, but I don't know your name," I said. "I'm Jessica."

"Trevor," he said.

"Trevor, do you mind if I ask you a few questions?"

"Shoot," he said.

I held up the pick I'd found at Ms. Minerva's. "Do you recognize this?"

He squinted at it. "It's one of our guitar picks," he said.

"Do you know who it belongs to?"

He shook his head. "No idea," he said. "It's a promotional item. We hand them out by the dozens."

A dead end.

"Sorry I couldn't help."

"Anything weird going on with the band?" I asked.

His easy smile disappeared. "Why do you ask?"

"Something happened?"

His answer wasn't what I expected. "I don't know what you heard, but that thing with Talulah Crank was blown way out of proportion. She and Scotty worked things out."

"Worked what out?"

"She wanted him to leave the band, go solo," he burst out. "Can you believe it? When he wouldn't, she went ballistic."

Could Talulah Crank be the one behind everything? Despite her icy demeanor, it didn't fit. She had a reputation for being good to her artists.

"Where's Scotty tonight?" I asked.

Trevor looked uncomfortable. "We don't really know, actually," he admitted. "But he's probably just sick. We're under lots of stress playing so often, you know?"

I thanked him and then went outside to find Flo's van, but it was already gone.

"I told her I'd give you a ride home," Dominic said, coming up behind me.

He didn't say anything during the ride, but abruptly pulled into the park instead of taking me home. The park looked different at night. The paths were deserted, the swings creaked from a slight breeze, and moonlight cast eerie shadows.

I shivered and turned my attention back to Dominic. "Did you want to talk to me about something? What's wrong?"

"You asked me if that song was prophetic," he said. "It was, but I can't figure out why."

"Does it mean anything to you?" I asked.

"Not a thing," he replied. "I've never sung it before. There is one thing, though. I sang one line twice."

"What was the line?"

"Something about the piper," he said. "I just don't get it."

"I think I do," I said. "When we were at the estate sale, the cashier mentioned that there was a rumor that the stolen flute had belonged to the Pied Piper of Hamelin."

"There aren't any children missing from Nightshade," he said.

"Well, there may be a musician missing," I said. "Drew Barrymore's Boyfriends don't seem to know where Scotty Turntable is. And then there are the injured musicians — Jeff Cool, and Sheila from Wet Noodles for Three. They didn't seem to know what they were doing when they hurt themselves. Maybe something is making them do it."

"Weird things started happening right after the estate sale. Maybe the estate sale company has some information about the stolen flute," he suggested. "Or maybe we can figure out the history of the flute some other way. Like the library."

I gave him an impulsive hug. "Brilliant idea. Let's start there."

He wrapped his arms around me and pulled me closer. We stayed like that for a long moment, but then from the side mirror, I caught sight of red lights flashing behind us.

"Not now," I groaned.

Dominic misunderstood me and moved away. "Sorry," he said in a hurt tone.

"It's not that," I said. "It's *that*." I pointed to the flashing lights.

There was a tap at the driver's side window. Then a flashlight was shone into the vehicle and I put up an arm to shield my eyes. The light moved away and I relaxed a bit.

"License and registration," the police officer said. I recognized that voice. Chief Wells. Great.

Dominic got some papers out of the glove box and handed them over.

"We weren't doing anything," I said defensively.

The flashlight came back my way. "Jessica Walsh,"

she said. "Why am I not surprised to see you? What are you two doing out past curfew?"

"I'm sorry, Chief Wells, I wasn't aware there was a curfew," Dominic said politely.

"I want you two to go home immediately." She handed the papers back to him.

"Yes, ma'am," Dominic said.

"No more late-night visits to the park," she said.

He started up the car and pulled away slowly.

"She made it sound like she caught us parking or something," I said.

"We were parking," he replied.

"No, we were parked," I said. "But we weren't doing anything wrong."

"Why are you so upset?" he asked. "It's no big deal."

"She basically told Teddie that she thinks I'm trouble," I told him. "And it bugs me."

"That's ridiculous," he said. "You protect Nightshade. There's nothing more noble than that."

"Tell that to Chief Wells," I replied.

"I will," he said.

I laid a hand on his arm. "Thanks, but it's not worth it. She's already made up her mind about me." The ironic part was that so had he. I was pretty sure I wasn't going to be changing either of their minds anytime soon.

CHAPTER TWELVE

I knew I was going to need to cram in as much practice as possible before the next round of Battle of the Bands. The chorus room was usually empty after school. I'd brought my guitar, the one Dominic had given me.

I heard whispering as I walked through the door. Harmony's back was to me, so she didn't see me walk in. She had what looked like sheet music clutched in her hands, but she appeared to be talking to herself.

She began to sing, and again I was blown away by how much her voice had improved. Her skill was increasing every day. Her sudden singing ability, combined with her cozy new friendship with Selena, made me suspicious.

She must have sensed my presence, because she whipped around and glared at me. "What are you doing here?"

I held up my guitar case. "I thought I'd practice."

The intensity of her glare diminished. "You can come back in a few minutes."

"I'll do that." I started to leave, but turned around to add, "You sound really good, Harmony. Great even."

She gave a tiny shrug. "It's not good enough. Have you ever wanted something so badly, something that feels out of your reach?" She didn't wait for me to answer. "I bet you haven't. I bet you get everything you want."

"Nobody gets everything they want. I certainly don't."

"That's not what it seems like," she said. Her desire to confide in me abruptly ended. She propped her music up on the piano and sat on the bench, her back to me again. It was a clear signal to leave, but I didn't.

She sang soft and low, in another language. It sounded like she was speaking German. I didn't understand the words, but the emotions were clear. She was singing about a lost love, someone she loved but who didn't love her back.

I could relate to that kind of rejection. I clapped loudly when she finished, but Harmony didn't even move.

I went around to the other side of the piano to face her. "I didn't know you spoke German."

She was so still. I felt like she was somewhere else. Literally. I waved a hand in front of her face, but she didn't even blink. The lights were on, but nobody was home.

"Harmony? Harmony!" She didn't answer me. I snapped my fingers. "Hey, wake up already."

She finally stirred. "W-w-what?"

"Are you okay?"

"I'm fine," she said. "Just a little tired. I've been practicing a lot. What were you saying again?"

"That I didn't know you spoke German."

"I don't," she said absently. Her mind was clearly on something else, but then she focused and her gaze sharpened. "Wait. What did you say?"

"The song," I spelled out. "It was in German."

"You heard wrong," she insisted.

I wasn't going to stand there arguing with her, and it was clear that she wasn't going to give up the choir room any time soon.

After leaving school, I went to the Nightshade public library to do some research about Mr. Lindquist's flute. Ms. Johns was at the reference desk, but her usual smile was missing.

"What can I help you with today?"

"Does the library have any information about the origins of the flute stolen from Mr. Lindquist?" I asked. "He said it was really rare."

"Mr. Lindquist?" Her face paled.

I nodded. "We wanted to try to help him get it back. I know it's a long shot."

"Then you haven't heard?"

"Heard what?" I was confused. She looked upset, but

119

what could I have said that would make her react that way?

"Mr. Lindquist died two days ago," she said. "The people from the moving company found him."

"I'm sorry to hear that," I said. "How did he die?"

"They're not saying."

I tried to absorb the news, but there was a sick feeling in my stomach. Something odd was going on. Mr. Lindquist was supposed to be in Florida by now, enjoying his retirement.

"When's the funeral?"

"Sunday afternoon," Ms. Johns said. She gave me the particulars of the service and as we said our goodbyes, she added, "And Jessica, the library has a couple of books about magical instruments." She wrote down the titles and pointed me in the right direction.

I decided to check out a book about the legend of the Pied Piper, along with a few others.

I came home with a stack of books, but I didn't get the chance to read any of them that night.

I wasn't looking forward to virago practice. Flo had excused me since I'd caved about joining Side Effects May Vary, but Raven had talked me into going anyway.

"I miss you," she said. "And besides, Flo said we're doing something special."

"Special" turned out to be virago boot camp, which was twice as hard as regular virago training. What made it worse was that the park was crowded with Hamlin fans.

After about a hundred planks, I called out, "I give!"

Andy managed about three more before she collapsed next to me.

After practice, we decided to have a quick breakfast at Slim's.

"Want to come with us, Flo?" I asked.

"I get enough of that place, thanks," she replied. "Besides, I'm having brunch with Hunter to celebrate. He sold a song to a record label, and a very famous singer is recording it."

Wishing powder, no doubt.

The thought made me lose my appetite, but only until we got to Slim's and I smelled his fresh cinnamon rolls. Brett Piper sat at a booth extremely close to Katrina Phillips, but a cute girl wearing a UC Nightshade tee walked by and he stared at her openly.

"That guy is a creep," Andy said.

I nudged her, and she looked abashed. "Sorry, Raven."

"It's okay," Raven said. "I think he's a creep too."

I stared at Brett. "What does she see in him?"

"I don't get it either," Raven said.

Brett felt us watching him and gave us a big wink. We all looked away hurriedly.

"Slim's having a karaoke night tonight," Andy said. "Isn't that exciting?"

"If you say so," Raven said. She didn't like the spotlight.

"It will be fun," Andy coaxed. "Everyone in Nightshade is going to be here. It's a fundraiser for Battle of the Bands."

"Isn't karaoke kind of nineties?" Raven asked.

"Exactly," Andy said. "That's why it will be fun. It's retro."

She was so excited about it, I couldn't say no. "I'm in," I said.

"And maybe you guys can spend the night at my house afterward?" Andy asked. She was a junior. There was no way the words "slumber party" were going to cross her lips.

"I'll ask Aunt Katrina, but I think she'll say yes," Raven said.

"It's got to be more fun than our last slumber party," I said. We'd spent the night nursing Eva, who'd been infected with a zombie virus. Speaking of which — "Can Eva come too?"

122

Andy nodded. "The more the merrier," she said. "I'm going to invite a couple of girls from my class."

Raven and I exchanged glances. Selena. It was Andy's party, after all. I tried to smile, but it took an effort. "Great."

CHAPTER THIRTEEN

My whole family decided to go to Slim's karaoke night. We took the enormous passenger van that we used to haul our entire family around.

We even had room for Eva. She and I helped unload the little ones while my sister Sarah acted all cool. Because she was in eighth grade, she thought she was too adult to hang out with the little kids.

As soon as we walked into the diner, she ran off to hang out with her best friend. Andy was sitting with Eva's sister Bethany, Bethany's best friend, Tiffany, and Selena, Harmony, and Raven. Dominic and his aunt were at a table next to them.

"Let's sit in the front," Katie said. She tugged on my hand and dragged me to a long table near the mike. The rest of the family followed.

"There are your friends," Mom said. "Why don't you go ahead and sit with them?"

Eva and I looked at each other. "We'll hang out with you guys for a while." Anything to avoid Bethany.

"Anybody hungry?" Dad asked. There was a chorus of yeses from my sisters.

After Flo took our order, Katie jumped up and ran over to Dominic. He grinned and gave a nod. He was so good with my little sister. The Giordanos sat at a table in the back, but Ryan wasn't there and neither was Rose's boyfriend, Nicholas. No Connor, either, which was kind of odd, since he was participating in Battle of the Bands.

A large noisy group walked into the diner, headed by the members of Hamlin. Brett was in the front of the pack and an adoring fan hung on each of his arms.

I shook my head. "Their fans never leave them alone."

Slim and his fiancée, Natalie, stood by the door greeting customers.

"Have you noticed anything different about Slim?" I asked Eva. Tonight, he was dressed in a dinner jacket and a hat and scarf that concealed most of his face and the fact that Slim was Nightshade's version of the invisible man.

"Not really," she said.

"He looks a little more solid than usual," I replied.

"Solid?" she asked.

"Like less invisible and more visible."

She stared at him until I nudged her to stop. "I think you're right," she said as he walked to the front of the crowd and took the microphone.

"Welcome to the first annual Slim's Diner Karaoke Night," Slim said. "All donations will go toward the grand prize for the Battle of the Bands event. Now, who wants to go first?"

The restaurant was full of Nightshade citizens, but nobody stepped up to the mike. "It's a fundraiser," Slim reminded the crowd.

Brett Piper, the lead singer from Hamlin, took the stage and snatched the microphone from Slim. Brett launched into a pitchy rendition of Whitesnake's "Here I Go Again," but the karaoke machine wasn't even on yet. Slim reached over and pushed the power button.

Brett continued to sing, but I noticed his fans seemed to lose interest after about the second out-of-tune Whitesnake song.

Eva nudged me. "The magic is gone." She was joking, but her comment made me think. Was Brett's allure solely a magical one? There were plenty of singers who needed Auto-Tuning to sound good, but his fans seemed slavishly adoring and I couldn't figure out why. Maybe magic was the answer?

Brett started on another song and there were audible groans from the audience. Slim eased the mike out of

Brett's hands. "Let's give a round of applause for Brett, everyone. You'll see his band, Hamlin, at round three of Nightshade's Battle of the Bands."

"How is it possible that they've made it this far?" I said.

There was a smattering of applause. Slim held out a large fishbowl with DONATIONS FOR BATTLE OF THE BANDS written on it, and Brett reluctantly dropped a couple of bills into it.

"Who would like to go next?" Slim asked. Nobody raised their hands, except, to my horror, my parents, who giggled like schoolgirls as they went up to the stage.

They made their selection from the karaoke list and then sang along to the words flashing on the TV screen next to them. They belted out "I Got You Babe," the old Sonny and Cher tune. Then Dad did a solo of "Sweet Caroline," which had the crowd roaring their approval. Caroline was my mom's first name and she got all misty-eyed as he sang it to her.

I'd forgotten how musical my parents were. They both sang in chorus when they were in high school, and Mom had even sung in college. Maybe that's why we all loved music, even my brother Sean, who couldn't carry a tune to save his life.

My parents got a standing ovation and then came back to our table. "That was fun," Mom said breathlessly.

"My turn," Katie said. She walked to the stage, followed by Dominic. They consulted the playlist and then sang "You've Got a Friend in Me," from *Toy Story*.

Next, Harmony stepped up to the mike and sang a super-melodramatic version of "The Rose." Eva rolled her eyes as Harmony ended with a really long note.

"You have to admit, she sounds really good," I said.

"Yeah," Eva replied. "Weird, isn't it?"

It was weird. "Do you think her mom paid for singing lessons?"

The next karaoke singers stepped up to the microphone. Ms. Johns and Harmony's mom sang "9 to 5," which drew a rousing round of applause.

By the time the night was over, Slim's had raised more than a thousand dollars for the Battle of the Bands grand prize.

After karaoke, we headed for Andy's. Harmony rode with Selena, who drove a sleek little white sports car that only fit two.

The rest of us rode with Andy, who parked in the street below. "Driveway's kind of steep," she explained. Selena parked behind Andy's car, and we all walked up the long driveway, carrying our sleeping bags.

Andy and her father lived in a little white house with

an ocean view. Moonlight lit the path to their house. To the right was a separate one-car garage with bougainvillea climbing up one wall. A basketball hoop hung above the garage door.

There were two chairs in front of the postage-stamp-sized front yard. "Your place is so cute," Raven said as we all entered. "Like a dollhouse."

"You can put your stuff in here," Andy said. Her bedroom looked like a pink and white powder puff. A pink gingham comforter covered a queen-sized bed and there was wall-to-wall fluffy white carpet. A high shelf, which wrapped around the entire room, was lined with porcelain dolls. Their unblinking stares creeped me out.

Andy noticed me looking at them. "They were my mom's."

"Your room is so pretty," Harmony raved.

"My dad hired an interior decorator," Andy said, "as a surprise."

The room didn't reflect her personality at all.

We set our sleeping bags down.

"What should we do now?" Andy said. She gave the bed a little bounce. Raven sat next to her and kicked off her shoes.

"Let's go down to the beach," Selena suggested.

"It's pretty late," Andy objected.

"What's the matter?" Selena asked. "Are you scared?"

She and Harmony broke into gales of laughter.

"I'm fine with staying here," I said. "The water is probably freezing."

Harmony rolled her eyes, imitating Selena. "Don't be such a baby, Jessica."

"Let's go," Raven said. She grabbed her shoes and put them back on.

"I'll get flashlights," Andy said. "I've heard there's a cave down there somewhere."

"Seems like the perfect time to go exploring," I said dryly. "After midnight. On a full moon. In Nightshade."

But they all had their shoes and jackets back on. I grabbed mine and followed behind them.

We tiptoed out the back door. "Which way?" Harmony asked in a loud voice.

"Shh, you'll wake up my dad," Andy said. She pointed to the wooden stairs going down the cliff to the beach.

We crept down to the sand. There was a lone figure walking along the surf toward us. His hoodie was up, which concealed most of his face, but there was something familiar about him. He seemed lost in thought and didn't notice us until we were close enough to recognize him.

"Hey, that's Connor," Andy said in a carrying voice. I

was walking a little bit ahead of the others and was almost upon him, but he didn't even seem to recognize the sound of his own name.

"Hi, Connor," I said. "What brings you out here tonight?"

His head whipped up and for a second, I saw panic in his eyes.

Something was wrong. "Connor, are you okay?" I asked. I took a step closer to him. "We missed you at karaoke tonight."

"Leave me alone, Jessica," he said. His voice was gravelly and rough, like he'd been gargling sand or something.

"Is something wrong?" I asked. "Is there something I can do?"

"Yeah, get away from me," he growled.

"Fine," I said. I stomped back to the others, who had held back to give us a moment of privacy. When I turned to look at him again, he was running up the beach in the direction he'd just come.

"That was weird," Eva commented.

"Boys can be so moody," Selena said.

I stared after Connor. "Yeah, especially during a full moon."

Selena was obviously already tired of the subject. "Where to now?"

"The caves are supposed to be over there somewhere."

Andy pointed the flashlight to a cliff about a hundred yards away. We walked along the sand, huddled against the wind that had just sprung up.

"If this was a slasher film, we'd be down here in our nighties, running from the murdering psycho," Eva said in a spooky tone of voice. She was more of a fan of old-school horror than those films about the victimized woman running in peril from the crazy killer.

"I'd like to see someone try it," Andy said.

Raven shuddered. "I don't know how people watch that stuff." Though she was a virago, Raven was appalled by violence.

We scrambled across the rocks near the tide pool to get to the cave entrance.

Selena slipped and I reached out a hand to steady her. "Thanks," she said. "I'm not exactly wearing the right shoes for this." Her cute wedges were soaked and sandy.

Harmony said, "Can't you just, you know?" She snapped her fingers.

"This isn't an episode of *Sabrina, the Teenage Witch*," Selena said harshly. Harmony stomped ahead of us. "Besides, I'm not using magic right now."

"You're not?" I asked. "But I thought that you'd . . ." I trailed off, realizing as I said the words how insulting they might seem.

"I'd what?" Selena asked. She didn't seem mad, just curious.

"Helped Harmony get in tune," I said in a low voice.

She shook her head. "Not me," she said. "But now that you mention it, she's really improved. You don't think she went somewhere else to get a little magical makeover, do you?"

"It's possible," I said. "Nobody could improve that much in such a short time."

"She's lost a lot of weight, too," Selena said. "And very quickly."

"Have you tried talking to her?" I asked.

Selena nodded. "She says she's fine, but she gets these headaches."

A lonely howl sounded in the distance. We stopped moving, waiting silently. An answering howl came a minute later, this one closer to us.

My sneakers squelched as I walked through the wet sand to the cave's entrance.

Andy stopped at the mouth and shone her flashlight into the darkness. There was a skittering noise and then the gleam of tiny eyes. "It's just a couple of rats," Andy said dismissively, but her voice shook. She walked into the cave. "Are you guys coming or not?" came floating back.

"Why are we doing this again?" Eva asked.

"Complete and utter stupidity," I said. Then I followed Andy into the cave. I gripped my flashlight tightly.

It was cold in the cave, and it had a peculiar odor.

"It smells horrible in here," Harmony commented. "Hold this for me." She handed me her flashlight and then wound a scarf more tightly around her neck. "I need to take care of the voice."

My foot crunched something and I shone my flashlight on the ground. I'd stepped on a small piece of plastic. I don't know why, but I picked it up and put it in the pocket of my hoodie.

There was a pile of trash in one corner and what looked like a pile of clothes against the low wall of the cave. My flashlight hit the shine of a hand sticking out from the ragged clothing.

That's when Harmony started to scream.

CHAPTER FOURTEEN

It was a young man in his early twenties. He looked like he was sleeping, but when I took a deep breath and then felt for a pulse, there wasn't one.

I whipped out my phone, but there was no reception. "Let's get out of here," I said. "We can call the police from Andy's house."

We climbed over the rocks and ran on the beach, up the steps, and toward Andy's. Harmony shrieked the entire time. Lights went on all over the neighborhood.

"Harmony, put a sock in it," Andy snapped. Harmony's shriek turned into a hiccupping sob.

"Andy? Where are you?" Her dad ran out of the house. He carried a baseball bat in one hand and his cell in the other.

"Over here, Dad," Andy said. "I'm so grounded," she added under her breath. "Can you call the PD? We found a dead body in the cave."

"What were you doing in the cave?" he asked. "I've

told you a hundred times that . . ." Then the rest of what she said sunk in, and he snapped open his cell phone and dialed.

The dead guy had been wearing a familiar-looking T-shirt. I tried to remember where I'd seen him before, but the memory escaped me.

When the police and coroner arrived, we all went back down to the beach to watch the action. The grownups weren't aware that I was eavesdropping. It was obvious they were too shaken up about the dead body to notice I was within listening distance.

"I think I recognize that young man," Mr. Bone said. "He performed the other day." I assumed Mr. Bone was here in an official capacity. He owned Mort's Mortuary.

"Who is he?" Officer Denton asked.

"I don't know his name," Mr. Bone replied. "But he plays — I mean played — for a band. I saw them at the mall the other day."

"That means," Chief Wells replied, "that the body has been here for" — she looked at Mr. Bone for confirmation — "less than five days."

"Any guesses about how he died?" Officer Denton asked.

"The body looks waterlogged," the chief observed. "Could have drowned."

From what I could see of him, the body didn't look drained of blood, so it couldn't have been vampires.

"Can I take the girls inside now?" Andy's dad interrupted.

The chief looked at Officer Denton. "Did we get contact information?"

"Yes, Chief," the officer replied.

She nodded. "Go ahead," she said. "And I'd suggest that in the future, you keep a closer eye on these girls. I will be."

She made us sound like juvenile delinquents. Which, fortunately, made Andy's dad less mad at us and madder at the chief.

"It's getting late," he said. "And I want to call their parents as soon as possible."

"I'll be in touch," Chief Wells said. It sounded like a threat.

We trudged back to the house. "What is it about us and slumber parties?" Raven finally said.

I couldn't help it. I giggled, despite the freakiness of the evening. Or maybe because of it. "At least we didn't run into anything with fangs or fur," I said. *Except maybe Connor*, I thought, but I wasn't going to share my suspicion with the group.

"Why don't you girls head to Andy's room," her dad

suggested. "It's late. Andy, I want to talk to you a minute. Alone."

We left them in the living room and went to Andy's room to change. When I took off my hoodie, the piece of plastic I'd found in the cave fell onto the carpet.

It was cracked, but still recognizable. A guitar pick. This one had a *B* and an *O* on it. The Black Opal? I put it in my overnight bag. Was it a clue or just coincidence? After all, the dead guy played in a band. Used to play in a band, I corrected myself, before someone killed him.

"I need a shower," Raven said. "I smell like cave."

I didn't blame her for wanting to wash off.

"I could use a shower too," Selena admitted.

"Help yourself," Andy said, strolling in. "My bathroom is right through that door."

"Can I go first?" Harmony suddenly said.

"Sure," Selena said.

"I'll put a movie on in the living room," Andy said. "What do you want to watch? Horror or cheesy romantic comedy?"

"Romantic comedy!" we said in unison. Finding the body had kind of ruined the idea of a scary movie. Even Eva was up for something light.

"Start the movie without me," Harmony said. "I'll be out in a few minutes."

We took our sleeping bags into the living room and Andy started the movie. We were a few minutes in when I realized I'd left my cell in Andy's bedroom and I'd promised Mom I'd check in. She'd probably already talked to Andy's dad and would be freaking out.

"I'll be right back," I said.

There was a humming noise coming from Andy's room. When I opened the door, Harmony was standing near the window. She had faded sheet music clutched in her hands. As I watched, she climbed out of the window onto the roof.

"Harmony?" I asked. "Harmony, what are you doing?" I followed her, but stopped at the window's ledge.

She didn't answer me, but started to sing a German song. She slipped and skittered down the roof. Her shirt snagged on something and it stopped her.

I stretched out and grabbed her. "A little help here!" I yelled.

Harmony didn't even flinch. She tried to wriggle from my grasp.

"Jessica, what's taking you so long?" Raven asked from the doorway.

"Get over here and help me," I said through gritted teeth.

"What are you doing?" I felt her peer over my shoulder. "Harmony!" she gasped.

"Grab her other arm," I ordered.

Raven was strong, stronger than me, and between the two of us, we managed to haul Harmony inside. We guided her to the bed and she sat docilely. She dropped the sheet music to the floor. She stared at a spot on the wall.

"What is wrong with you, Harmony?" Raven asked.

"She was singing in German again," I said. I had told my fellow viragos about what I had seen that day in the chorus room.

Harmony was shivering and Raven draped a blanket around her shoulders.

"Where am I?" Harmony asked. The dazed look was leaving her eyes. "I thought we were going to watch a movie."

Raven and I exchanged glances. There wasn't much we could do to help her tonight, but we could keep her away from the sheet music. When Harmony wasn't looking, I slid the music into my back pocket.

"You're right," I finally said. "Let's go watch a movie. Raven, why don't you take her downstairs." Raven gave me a look as she escorted Harmony out of the room.

When they were gone, I took a closer look at the sheet music. Sure enough, it was the same piece that Harmony had snatched out from under me at the estate sale. I supposed I should be glad I didn't get it, since it seemed to have some kind of evil power. It felt electric in my hand. I didn't want to take a chance on Harmony doing anything else dangerous, so I took a breath, went to the window, and tossed the sheet music out. I watched as it was whisked down to the beach on the chilly night breeze. Then I closed the window and went downstairs to join the other girls.

CHAPTER FIFTEEN

Eva and I had volunteered to help collect donations at the high school's recycling drop-off on our lunch break. We sat at a little table at the end of the parking lot. There was a tiny canopy over it to shade us.

"Did you hear?" she asked me.

"Hear what?" Whatever it was, Eva was positively bursting to tell me.

"They identified the body we found," she said. "It was Scotty Turntable."

I finally realized where Mr. Bone had seen him. "From Drew Barrymore's Boyfriends," I said. "I knew he looked familiar."

"What do you think will happen to the band now?" she asked. "Will they have to drop out of the Battle of the Bands?"

"I don't know," I said. "Did you hear anything about how he died?"

She shook her head. "Nope. Not one word."

Over the course of our shift, a sizable pile of donated cans and bottles accumulated behind us.

Eva yawned. "Did you finish the history homework yet?" she asked me idly.

I started to answer her, but then my tattoo began to burn. I glanced at my bicep and the whirlwind circled furiously. I looked around, but the parking lot was empty. There wasn't even a cloud in the sky.

A rustling sound came from the pile of aluminum cans behind us, followed by a strange scratching noise. "What is that?" Eva asked. She reached over and grabbed the bag in question. It started to squirm.

"Eva, don't open that!" I said. But it was too late.

A stream of rats burst out of the plastic bag and one climbed onto Eva's arm. Her scream rang through the parking lot.

"Get it off me! Get it off me!"

I shuddered, but managed to knock the rat off her arm. But others still emerged from the plastic bag, each one bigger than the last.

"My phone," Eva cried. "Get my phone!"

I did as she asked. She grabbed it from me and hit a button. "I've got to get a shot of this." She continued to record while I watched her in disbelief.

"Can you believe it?" she said. "It's like something out of *Ben*." *Ben* was this horror movie from the seventies.

I was pretty sure Eva had seen every horror movie ever made. Which meant that I'd seen three-fourths of all the horror movies ever made.

A strange lilting song caught my ear. It came from somewhere behind the school building. "Did you hear that?" I asked.

"Hear what?" Eva said, still absorbed in filming the rodents, who scampered up the pile of recyclables.

Dominic and Evan came running from the boys' locker room. "We heard a scream. Everything okay?" Dominic asked.

"Everything's fine, if you don't count the rats," I replied.

"Rats? What rats?" Evan asked.

I looked around. The rodents had simply vanished.

Evan and Eva had their heads together while she showed him the little bit of footage she'd managed to take.

Dominic looked at his feet for a long minute. "How have you been?" he finally asked.

"Fine," I said, but there was an edge to my voice. His head whipped up.

"Jessica, I wanted to say something to you," he said. "But I haven't had the nerve."

"What's wrong with right now?"

He glanced at Eva and Evan, who held hands as

they watched the clip of the rats over and over again. He blushed and looked down. He clearly didn't think now was a good time. But I didn't have time for his stalling.

"I should call Flo," I said abruptly. "She'll want to know about the rats."

"Let's go, Evan," Dominic said. "We'd better get back or Coach will wonder where we are."

They took off at a run back to the gym. "Coach?" I looked at Eva for clarification.

"Didn't you know?" she asked. "Dominic tried out for track. He's on the team with Evan. They have a meet tonight so they must be practicing during lunch."

I had a hard time picturing Dominic on the team. He could run, I knew. He had the right build for it: long legs, muscular, broad shoulders.

"It doesn't seem like something Dominic would be into," I said.

"Maybe not rocker boy Dominic," Eva replied. "But there's more to him than that, right?"

"Right." There was definitely more to Dominic than just music. I was dreamily thinking of all of his good qualities when Eva said, "I thought you had to call Flo."

"I do!" I picked up the phone and dialed Flo. When she answered, I told her what happened.

"Rats, huh?" she said. "I'll let the Nightshade City Council know."

Fortunately, Eva and I were the last shift for recycling duty. We put the bag of recyclables into the storage shed, very carefully, but there wasn't even a squeak.

As we closed up, I noticed Hunter Verrat and Mitch Peverell leaving the school.

I nudged Eva. "Wonder what they were doing here."

She shrugged. "Probably a Battle of the Bands meeting. Ms. Clare is on the committee, after all."

"Maybe," I said. I didn't like Hunter or Mr. Peverell and I didn't know why. But why would Mitch Peverell be there if he wasn't even a judge?

Eva convinced me to go to the track meet that afternoon.

"I'll have to meet you there," I said. "I have to pick up Katie first. I promised my mom I'd watch her while she takes Kellie and Grace to gymnastics class."

"Katie will love it," Eva said. "She'll get a chance to see Dominic."

Eva was right. Katie practically tore my arm off in her excitement. "C'mon, Jessica," she said. "Quit walking so slow. We're going to miss it."

"Miss what?" I asked. "The track meet is like eight hours long."

"But Dominic's race is soon," she whined. "And I want to see him."

I did too but I wasn't going to say it aloud. I liked him, but did I like him enough to give him another chance to kick me to the curb the next time a chupacabra took a bite out of me?

When we reached the Nightshade High track, Dominic and Evan were stretching out on the grass, but they both sat up and waved when they saw us.

Later, as I watched Dominic hand off the baton to Evan in the relay, I told Eva, "He's getting faster." Dominic and I had gone on a few runs together.

"Why didn't you try out for track?" Eva asked.

"You know," I said cryptically. "My extracurriculars are already too much."

"You're so fast, though," she persisted.

"I get plenty of running in," I said. "You know, on Saturday mornings."

The light finally dawned on her. "Oh, yeah," she said. "I almost forgot about the virago thing."

I nudged her hard and glanced meaningfully at Katie.

"She's not even paying attention," Eva said.

"I'm not paying attention about what?" Katie said, her eyes still glued on the runners.

"Nothing, kiddo," I said.

The boys' relay was over. The Nightshade team came in second place.

Evan and Dominic did their cooldown stretches and then joined us on the bleachers.

Evan greeted Eva with a long kiss. Dominic and I stared everywhere but at the kissing couple.

When they finally finished their lip-lock, Evan said, "Hey, Dom, do you guys want to catch a movie with us tonight? We'll even let Jessica pick."

Eva elbowed him in the ribs.

"Sounds good to me," Dominic replied easily. "Jessica?"

I was so mad. He was pretending like we were still a couple. But that was something he was going to have to discuss with me first.

"I have to babysit Katie tonight," I said shortly.

"No you don't," Katie said. I hadn't thought she was paying attention to the conversation, but clearly she was.

"Yes, I do," I said. "In fact, it's time for us to go home." I stomped down the stairs. Katie followed me slowly. Dominic Gray was the most insensitive, clueless . . .

"Jessica, wait!" he said.

"Why don't you call me when you make up your mind," I snapped. "You broke up with me, remember? You can't just pretend that it didn't happen."

"I'm not," he said. "I was too chicken to ask you out again, so I convinced Evan to . . ."

"Do your dirty work for you?" I suggested.

"Something like that," he said.

"Well, it's not going to work," I said. "If you want to go out with me, you're going to have to prove to me that you're not going to change your mind again and dump me just like you did last time."

"I can do that," he said.

"And Dominic, the next time you want to go out with me, ask."

"I can do that, too," he replied.

I marched off without looking back.

CHAPTER SIXTEEN

Following our midweek after-school run, Raven, Andy, Flo, and I were sitting around the kitchen table at the Mason house drinking sodas when Hunter came in.

"Flo," he chirped, "I just got a new car. Want to go for a ride?"

Flo's face lit up. "Sure," she said. "You don't mind that I'm all sweaty, do you?"

Hunter's nose wrinkled. "We can put down a towel or something." He shot the three of us a dirty look as they left through the back door.

As soon as we heard his car pull away, I said, "Do we have time to do any snooping?"

Andy pulled a yearbook from her gym bag. "Already started. It's the yearbook from Flo's junior year at Nightshade High. I got it from the library." She flipped through until she found the page she'd been looking for.

"Hunter Verrat and his pet Wilbur," Raven read over Andy's shoulder.

"Flo never even mentioned that Hunter had a pet rat," I said. "Even when I told her about the rats in the recycling."

"Exactly," Raven said. "Flo's too loyal to Hunter to be suspicious, but I smell a rat." She giggled at her own pun.

"Do you think he's the one who sent those rats to attack you and Eva?" Andy asked. "Or took the wishing powder? Or both?"

"I think it's time we found out," I whispered. "Let's search his room."

We crept upstairs and pushed open the door to Hunter's room. It was tidy, but stark. There were no photos or personal items. I crossed to the desk. The pens and papers were lined up with precision, but when I opened the center drawer, a blue smudge caught my eye.

"Come look at this," I told them. "The powder was definitely here."

"Shh," Raven said. "Do you hear that?"

"What?" I whispered. We didn't move and after a second, I heard a faint squeaking noise.

Andy followed the sound and stood in front of the closet. She put an ear to the door. "It's coming from in here."

"Don't open it!" Raven shouted, but it was too late. Andy turned the handle and dozens of rats streamed from the closet.

They left the bedroom, but that didn't stop me from screaming at the top of my voice when a rat scrambled over my foot.

Dominic came running. "Jessica, are you okay?" he asked.

"*We* are fine," Andy said dryly. "Thanks for asking."

"What are you doing here, anyway?" I asked.

"I thought you girls could use a ride home after training," he said.

"Any excuse to drive your new car," Raven muttered.

"Hey, sis, it's gotten you plenty of places," Dominic said. Raven smiled.

We walked out to the driveway. Just then, a hunter green Jaguar zipped down the street with Hunter at the wheel. "Boys and their cars," said Andy as she climbed into the back seat of Dominic's Honda.

As we drove, Raven said, "Dominic's got some big news, Jessica. Band news."

Dominic gave his sister a look. "It's not that big."

"Spill it!" I said.

"That talent agent is interested in the band," he said. "He's been to a couple of our shows, but I don't know."

"Did you tell Katrina and Vinnie know?" I asked.

Dominic nodded. "The band would have to talk about it, of course. And I don't know how legit he really is," he admitted. "His business card is a guitar pick."

"A guitar pick?"

"Cheesy, right?" Dominic said. "He collects them."

"Are you talking about Mr. Peverell?" I asked.

Dominic nodded. He didn't seem that excited about it. "There's something about him that I don't like. Anyway, I'm meeting with him tonight."

"Let me know how it goes," I said.

"I will."

I got the feeling Dominic still wanted to talk to me about our relationship, but we couldn't with the others in the car, so I just made small talk.

"Where did you learn to drive?" I asked.

"My dad," he said. "He taught me to be a careful driver. I've never forgotten it."

I watched him drive away when he dropped me off.

"Jessica, we need you to watch your sisters tonight," Mom said as soon as I walked in the door.

"Hello to you, too," I said, but under my breath.

Mom and Dad had some school thing at the middle school with Sarah and Sydney, but promised to be back before ten.

While my sisters played in the family room, I took

the opportunity to dig into my library books and read up on the Pied Piper.

What I learned fascinated me. The Pied Piper legend was hundreds of years old. The German town of Hamelin had refused to pay the piper after he had fixed their rat problem by leading them away with his music. In retaliation, he played his pipe again and rounded up all the children of Hamelin and led them to parts unknown.

One book theorized that the musical pipe actually existed and had been handed down in secrecy from generation to generation. The music it played was a spell, a song that could make anyone do whatever the piper wanted.

A Pied Piper could also be someone who made wild promises. Who did that sound like?

After I had been reading for a while, the doorbell rang. I peeked out the keyhole and saw Connor standing on my front door.

I opened it. "Connor? What are you doing here?"

"I wanted to talk to you about something," he said. "Can I come in?"

He followed me into the living room where Katie, Kellie, and Grace were watching television. "Can we go somewhere a little more private?"

Private?

"I have six sisters, Connor," I said. "There is no such thing as privacy."

He wasn't going to say anything with an audience. "Let's go to the kitchen," I said. "But I'm babysitting, so you have five minutes."

Was he going to ask me out again? I didn't know what I would say. He'd definitely upped the magnetism quota since last fall, and the way he'd sung to me on my birthday was making me take a second look. Maybe we were both finally on the same page at the same time? Or maybe he was going to explain his weird behavior the night we found the body?

"I wanted to apologize to you," he said. "I snapped at you that night on the beach and I'm sorry."

"It's okay," I said.

"It's not okay," he said earnestly. "It was rude and I'm sorry."

"You're forgiven," I replied.

I waited for him to say something else, but instead he fiddled with the apples that my mom always kept in a bowl on the counter.

"I'd better get back to my sisters," I finally said.

"Wait!" he said. "There's something else. I gave it my all on your birthday. Big romantic gesture and everything.

But I sang you a song and he gave you a guitar." We both knew who he was talking about.

"I loved your song," I said softly.

He shrugged. "I know when I'm beat," he said. "It's time for me to move on."

We were definitely not on the same page. Maybe not even in the same book.

"But I —" I started to say, but then changed my mind. "I understand."

"I wanted to talk to you about something else," he said. "I wanted to tell you in person so you wouldn't be caught off-guard if someone else mentioned it."

"Off-guard?" What was he going to tell me?

"I know you and Selena aren't the best of friends, but she and I have grown closer since we started the band," he said.

Wait. Connor was dating Selena? She was a junior and he was a sophomore, but they had music in common. Maybe he would balance her out a little.

Connor was still talking, and I realized I'd lost track of the conversation.

"So we're friends?" he said. "You're not upset?"

"Not at all, Connor," I said. "I hope you and Selena are very happy."

As I walked him to the door, I wondered. I didn't really hope that. For a tiny, mean-spirited second, I'd hoped that they would break up immediately. What was wrong with me? I didn't have Dominic, and suddenly Connor was appealing?

CHAPTER SEVENTEEN

The next morning, Eva and I met at our usual spot. She rushed up, out of breath. "You'll never believe what Selena told me this morning," she said.

My mind was still on the Piper lore I'd learned the night before. "What?" I said absently.

"Connor and Dominic got caught drag racing last night."

"Dominic would never race his car," I said. "I don't believe it."

When I ran into Dominic at his locker, I asked him, "Is it true?"

He slammed his locker shut. "Is what true?" He wouldn't look at me.

"That you and Connor were drag racing?"

He nodded.

"Of all the stupid, dangerous stunts."

"You aren't telling me anything I haven't already told myself," he said.

"Then why did you do it?" I threw the question over my shoulder as I walked away, but then something made me stop. Why *would* Dominic do something so out of character?

I walked back to where he stood. "Tell me exactly what happened," I ordered.

"I had a meeting with Mitch Peverell," Dominic said. "As I was leaving, Connor showed up."

"How'd your meeting go?" I asked, momentarily diverted.

"He made a lot of promises," Dominic said wryly. "And he kept talking about Hamlin and how great they were. He wanted me to stay to listen to their music, but I told him I had to leave."

"That's weird," I said.

"Anyway, I pulled up to a stoplight, Connor was in the car next to mine, and the next thing I knew, we were racing. If Poppy Giordano hadn't been nearby and stopped us using her telekinesis, we would have driven straight off a cliff."

I shuddered. "That's all you remember?"

"We were listening to music," he said. "A killer tune." He rummaged in his bag and produced a CD. "Mr. Peverell gave me this at the meeting."

I gasped. "Dominic, this is a Hamlin CD!" The album cover consisted of a shadowy figure playing a very familiar-looking flute. The audience was made up of rats instead of people. One of the rats even had a cell phone in his hand.

"That's Mr. Lindquist's flute," I said. Dominic looked confused, as if he was just waking up and wasn't sure where he was. "But I hate Hamlin," he said. "That's what I was listening to? I can't stand that Brett guy."

"Brett, that's it!" I said. "I can't believe I didn't see it before."

"See what?"

"Don't you get it?" I asked. "Brett *Piper*. The name of his band is Hamlin. I think they're using some kind of magical music to lead people to their doom. That's what they tried to do to you. You've got to tell your aunt to stay away from Brett, or else."

The bell rang and we headed to class, but Dominic's words nagged at me all day. *A killer tune.* What if the Pied Piper was using music to kill off the competition?

After my last class, I headed for Slim's. Raven and Andy were waiting for me outside the diner.

"Where's Flo?" I asked. I couldn't wait to tell her what I'd found out about the piper.

"Vinnie's disappeared," Raven said.

"Vinnie is really missing?" I asked. Maybe the Piper had gotten to him and it was too late.

Andy nodded. "Flo went looking for him."

"Why aren't we helping her?" I asked.

"She took off without telling us where she was going," Raven explained. "Flo's freaking out after the stuff happening to bands in Nightshade."

"She wasn't thinking clearly," Andy said. "I've never seen her so upset."

"Did Flo mention hearing any strange music?" I asked.

Andy snorted. "She's a virago and she dates a musician," she said. "She probably hears strange music all the time."

She had a point.

"Let's sit down and see if we can figure something out."

Slim's was packed. Natalie was waiting tables and Daisy was in the kitchen. She flipped pancakes with a little help from her psychic skills. She turned around for a second and caught me watching and gave me a wink before she returned to her task.

Natalie took our orders and then we resumed our conversation. I told them my theory about Brett Piper being behind the strange things that happened to the musicians.

"I think you're on to something," Raven said. "My Aunt Katrina definitely has the weird obsessive thing going on with Brett. And that's not like her at all."

"It's like she's under his spell," Andy said. "What exactly was that myth about the Pied Piper about, anyway? Maybe there's a clue in it about why he's doing this."

"Revenge," I said. "It's about revenge. The Piper drove the rats from Hamelin and when the townspeople didn't pay him as promised, he took their children."

"What were the titles of the songs Dominic sang?" Raven asked. "Dom's pretty good about providing clues, even if he doesn't know what they mean."

"True," Andy said.

"He sang 'Promises, Promises,'" I said. "And 'Masquerade.' And then when he sang 'Stairway to Heaven,' he repeated the line about the piper."

"Dominic really hit the nail on the head this time, psychically speaking," Raven said. "He practically drew us a picture. The Pied Piper is back and he's in Nightshade."

"We need to find out everything we can about Brett Piper and his band, Hamlin," Raven said. "But first, we have to find Vinnie before he gets hurt."

We asked Natalie for our check, but she shook her head. "On the house," she said. "It's the least I can do after you have done so much work on our house."

"The house!" I said. "Did anyone think to check at the Mason house? Maybe Vinnie is there. He could be hurt."

"It's a possibility," Natalie admitted. "Vinnie's been helping out, too." She handed me a key. "Why don't you guys go check? But be careful."

Andy drove us to the Mason house. "There's no sign of Vinnie's car," she said.

"Let's check it out anyway," I said.

The house was dark. After I entered the front door, I turned on the light switch, but it was dead.

"I'll get a flashlight from the car," Andy said.

When she returned with the light, we moved forward. I heard a noise coming from another room and then froze, but the sound stopped.

"Do you think it's rats?" Raven asked. She moved closer to us. I shuddered, remembering the rats in the Hunter's closet.

"Why is the electricity off?" I asked.

A vaguely familiar voice answered me. Hunter. "We are in the middle of a remodel," he said.

Had he been standing there watching us?

"What are you doing here?" I asked.

"I'm staying here, remember?" he said. "Flo called me a few minutes ago and asked me to turn off the power."

It was a rat all right. A songwriter rat.

"But . . ." Raven started to say something, but I gave her a quick nudge and she stopped.

It was highly unlikely Flo had called him in the middle of our search for her missing boyfriend. Which meant he was lying through his capped teeth.

His gaze kept drifting back in the same direction.

There was obviously something in the den that he didn't want us to see.

"What are you doing here?" Hunter asked.

"Natalie sent us," I said. "We're looking for something."

Some*one*, I amended silently. I didn't trust Hunter enough to tell him anything.

"What does she want?" he asked. He moved in front of the den's doorway.

Raven and Andy were catching on that something was up. "It is her house," Raven pointed out.

"Yes, yes, of course," he said, but he didn't budge. He draped an arm across the doorway. It was an outwardly casual pose, but I ducked under his arm and into the room.

"You can't go in there!" Hunter said.

"I'm already in," I said. When I surveyed the room, I was shocked. The room was empty, but there were so many holes punched into the wall that it looked like Swiss cheese.

Raven and Andy followed me. "What happened in here?" Raven asked.

"I told you," Hunter said. "I'm working."

"I don't remember Flo saying anything about tearing down walls," I said. "I thought you were staying here as a paying guest, anyway."

The holes were symmetrical and careful, not the kind of holes you made if you were renovating. He'd been hunting for something, but what?

Hunter's eyes shifted to a large gap in the wall, near the window. Whatever he had been looking for, I was almost sure he'd found it.

He stepped in front of me when I tried to move forward, but Raven was quicker than I was and darted to the hole before he could stop her.

"This is what you've been looking for the entire time," she said. She held up a large bag of indigo wishing powder.

"I thought the old witch had hidden more of that stuff," Hunter said. "And I was right."

"This belongs to Natalie," Raven said. "Not you."

"Be careful with that," Hunter said. "It's worth a small fortune." As he reached for it, Andy swatted his hand away, then grabbed his wrists and tied them behind his back.

When I raised my eyebrows in surprise that she had rope with her, she just shrugged and said, "A virago is always prepared."

I turned to our prisoner. "You're not Flo's friend. You're a thief."

"I don't understand," Raven said. "I thought he was a famous songwriter."

"He is a songwriter," I told her, "but he also steals whatever he can find."

He had the sense to look abashed. "I need it," he said. "I hadn't written a hit song in two years before I found that wishing powder in the attic. My career was going nowhere."

"So you did steal the wishing powder from my house," I replied.

"You were wasting it," he snarled. "Flo was stupid enough to tell me where you lived. I walked right in and helped myself. But it's already gone."

I moved forward until our noses almost touched. "Don't ever call Flo stupid again," I said.

"Or what?"

"Or you'll be in jail so fast your head will spin," I said.

"Are you the Pied Piper?" Raven asked.

I could understand her line of thinking. Hunter was a songwriter, had no compunction about dabbling in magic, and, most important, was desperate.

"What are you talking about?" Hunter asked.

"The rats?" Raven prompted. "Your pets."

"Rats?" Hunter said. "I haven't had a pet rat since high school."

His closet had been full of rats. "I'll be right back," I said. Andy handed me the flashlight, and I made my way down the hall to the guest room. The closet door was open and I approached it gingerly.

I shone the light in the closet. At first, I didn't see anything, but then I noticed a hole the size of my fist in the back of the closet. The rats could have come through there.

I went back to the others in the hallway. "Do you know what's next to your room?" I asked Hunter.

"Yeah," he said. "Mitch's room. You may think I'm scum, but I don't use rats to scare people."

We tried the door to Mr. Peverell's room, but it was locked.

"What should we do with Hunter?" Andy asked. The way she said it made me think she had a few things in mind.

"Call the police," I said. "Let them decide."

I knew that Flo would be hurt by his actions. I wasn't sure she could take the added humiliation of having everyone know he'd betrayed her trust.

Officer Denton answered the phone and came right over. I have to admit I felt a certain sense of satisfaction seeing Hunter escorted into the squad car.

"What should we do with this?" Raven asked, gesturing to the bag of powder.

"It's Natalie's," I said. "She and Slim could sell it and take a really nice honeymoon."

"Or at least patch up all these holes," Andy commented.

She was right. The house was a complete disaster.

I picked up a broom. "Let's get busy."

CHAPTER EIGHTEEN

Saturday was the day of the Battle of the Bands finals, and Vinnie was still missing. But the show must go on. A bunch of us were making posters for the event. Selena, Harmony, Andy, Raven, and I were all at Selena's house with markers and poster board galore.

Selena's room was immaculate, all white. It looked like an upscale hotel room. Even the carpet was white, so we'd taken off our shoes before we entered. The morning was chilly, so she had a toasty fire roaring in her fireplace.

"Where is everyone else?" Raven asked. "It's so quiet here."

Selena looked amused. "Sleeping," she said. "My aunt is married to a vampire, remember?"

"Oh, yeah," Raven said sheepishly.

"We can work on the floor," Selena suggested. "We'll have more room that way."

I was horrified. "What if we get marker on the carpet?"

She laughed. "Don't worry," she said. "If I can get bloodstains out, I can get a few marker stains out."

I didn't ask what that meant.

Andy handed out markers and poster board. Harmony hummed as she worked, but when I looked over at her poster, she'd written HELP ME in big block letters.

"You guys," I whispered. "Something's wrong with Harmony."

Harmony pitched forward and collapsed.

"She fainted!" Andy said.

"Get a washcloth and wet it with cold water," I said. "And let's move her to the bed."

Harmony was unconscious, but breathing. We put her on the bed and covered her with a blanket.

"She's been singing in German again," Selena said.

"What? But I threw the sheet music away," I told them.

"She got it back somehow," Selena said. "I saw her with it yesterday."

"We need to find that music and get rid of it once and for all," Andy said. She rummaged through Harmony's bag. "It's not in here."

"Where would she keep it?" Raven asked.

"Somewhere close to her," I said. "Check her pockets."

After a moment, Raven held up the sheet music. "What should I do with it?"

Either Harmony found the sheet music or the sheet music was finding Harmony. I wasn't sure which it was, but there was only one thing to do.

"Burn it," I said. I gave Selena a questioning look and she nodded.

Raven threw it into the fireplace and a sickly green glow emanated from it. We watched as the edges caught and then burned. Finally, there was nothing left but ashes.

Harmony sat up and put a hand to her head. "What happened?"

"I've seen spells like this," Selena said. "That sheet music must have been feeding off of you somehow." Harmony had been wasting away, losing so much weight.

"Try to sing, Harmony," I told her.

A few sickly notes came out of her mouth. I'd never been so happy to hear out-of-tune singing.

"You're back!" Selena cried happily. "I don't care if you can't sing a note." She gave Harmony a hug. It was the most emotion I'd ever seen Selena display.

"How are you feeling?" Andy asked.

"Like I've missed out on something," Harmony said.

"Don't you remember?" Selena asked.

"The last thing I remember was the estate sale," Harmony replied. "I have a gigantic headache. Anyone have any aspirin?"

Raven handed over some Tylenol and an unopened bottle of water. Harmony took it and a few minutes later, the color slowly returned to her cheeks.

"What are we going to do about the competition?" Harmony asked. "There's no way we'll win when I sound like my normal self."

We'd been so worried about her, we hadn't thought what it would mean for their band, Magic and Moonlight.

"Connor has a great voice," I said. "Maybe he could sing?"

Selena narrowed her eyes at me. I hoped she wasn't going to be snarky just because I'd mentioned Connor's name. She surprised me when she gave me a small smile. "Great idea, Jessica. And Harmony, do you feel up to playing guitar instead?"

"I know all the songs," Harmony admitted.

"Harmony plays something like twenty instruments," Selena bragged. "She's almost as good of a drummer as I am."

"That gives me an idea," I said. "Harmony, I have a big favor to ask you."

After the posters were finished, Eva and I stopped by Slim's to ask Natalie if there had been any word about

Flo and Vinnie. To my horror, the diner was closed. The big bay window was boarded up and there were shards of glass on the sidewalk. I picked them up and put them in the trash.

Officer Denton pulled up in his squad car as I was leaving.

"What happened here?" I asked.

"A bunch of Hamlin fans went berserk and trashed the place," he said. "It's a wreck inside. They won't be able to open up again for at least a week."

"Are Slim and Natalie okay?" Eva asked.

"Shaken up a bit," he said. "But they're more worried about Flo."

"We should help clean up," Eva said.

"We will," I assured her. "But first, we have to get to the park." This round of the Battle of the Bands was held outdoors at the city park.

When we arrived, they announced that Hunter Verrat was no longer able to participate as a judge. He would be replaced by Professor Carmine, a semi-retired music professor at UC Nightshade.

The judges were sitting at a table front and center to the stage.

It was exciting. They'd narrowed it down to ten bands, and the finalists had been assigned slots at random, so Hamlin was performing first. Side Effects May

Vary, which I guess meant *us* now, would be performing at seven on Saturday night.

Dominic peered over my shoulder at the list. "That's the best performance slot," he said with satisfaction.

"Do you really think we stand a chance?" I asked. "Jeff is a much more experienced performer than I am."

"I don't think Jeff loves music anymore," Dominic said. "He just loves the attention. That wouldn't get us any points from the judges. We're better off with you, so don't be nervous. Okay?"

He gave me a little sideways hug. I hugged him back. "Okay."

While we talked, Brett Piper rushed by. "Has anyone seen my guitar?"

Another missing instrument? It could be a coincidence, but my curiosity was piqued.

"Let's help Brett find his guitar," I said. I grabbed Dominic's arm and dragged him along with me.

Brett shouted at the poor guy who was their roadie. "What do you mean, you haven't seen it? It's your job to look after the equipment."

"Brett, it was here a minute ago," the guy replied.

"It's not here now!" Brett screamed. "Hal, I can't go on without my guitar. Now find it!"

"On second thought," I said, "Brett can find his own guitar."

I wondered if Brett's guitar was magic too. Come to think of it, I'd never seen him playing that magic flute that the Piper used.

The public library was adjacent to the park, so they'd temporarily converted offices into dressing rooms for the bands. Musicians were crammed into every available space.

"Do you want to hang out and catch some of the other bands?" Dominic asked.

"Are you asking me as a band mate or as a date?" I replied.

"Both, I guess," he said. "I want to spend time with you and I want to hear what you think of the other bands."

"Then lead on," I said.

Dominic took a quick look at the schedule. "Drew Barrymore's Boyfriends are up next," he said.

"Even without Scotty?" I said. "That seems harsh."

"I know," Dominic agreed. "But the rest of the band is convinced that Scotty would have wanted them to play."

"It's so sad, though."

He nodded. "It is. Want to get something to eat and then check them out? I think they're our biggest competition."

We walked to a food kiosk for a quick snack, then headed back to the stage to watch the performance.

Drew Barrymore's Boyfriends had just started their

set. Trevor announced that the first song was a tribute to Scotty Turntable, who'd tragically drowned. It was called "Couldn't Even Swim" and was a lament about how confusing Scotty's death was, considering he usually went to great lengths to avoid water.

Brett Piper from Hamlin was sitting on a blanket on the lawn, surrounded by a bunch of college girls.

DBBF did two original songs and then a cover of a Go-Go's song, which was an interesting choice for them. The crowd's applause was loud and long.

When it finally died down, Dominic said, "That's what I thought. They're the band to beat."

A song began to play in the distance. One of the other bands was probably warming up, but there was something about the melody that sent a chill through me.

Trevor, the lead singer of Drew Barrymore's Boyfriends, was surrounded by fans, but the mob was no longer friendly. There were screams and shouts and then Trevor disappeared from view.

Two girls tugged on his arms like he was a wishbone while another one grabbed his shirt and ripped it off him.

"I think Trevor needs help," I said. Then I was up and in the middle of the group of girls. "Break it up!" I said. "What is wrong with you people?"

They wouldn't listen to me. A tall brunette reached over and pulled out a chunk of his hair, which had to hurt.

Dominic had joined me. "Jessica, we need to get him out of here!" he yelled. "They're out of control."

I stood in front of Trevor while Dominic hauled him to his feet. The fans rushed us again, but I managed to block them.

"I think it's the music," I said. "They won't stop as long as that music is playing."

"Where's it coming from?" Dominic asked.

Trevor climbed on top of a picnic table and stood there. We climbed up after him. His lip was bleeding and he looked somewhat dazed. A few of the fans still tried to reach him.

"Where's security?" Dominic asked. "There's got to be some bouncers here, with a crowd this size."

I pointed to a big guy who had one of Trevor's feet and was tugging off his shoe. "He *is* security. We've got to get Trevor out of here," I said. "Or stop the music."

"You take him to my car," Dominic said. He tossed me his car keys. "I'll find out where the music is coming from and meet you there." He jumped off the picnic table and shouldered his way through the crowd.

People were swarming us as the music continued to grow more ominous by the second. I was afraid we wouldn't make it to the car if we left the relative safety of the picnic table.

A girl with pink streaks in her hair and long fake

fingernails jumped up on the table. She clawed at Trevor's face, but I blocked her and then shoved her to the ground.

A tall guy in a beanie and ripped jeans reached for Trevor's leg and tried to drag him off the table. I kicked him until he lost his grip, but he and the rest of the fans kept coming. I couldn't figure it out. It was a seemingly random outbreak of violence. These people were determined to hurt Trevor and I was determined to stop them.

The crowd started throwing anything they could get their hands on — food, full soda cans, and even a beach chair, which I managed to grab and use as a defensive weapon.

I thought about making a break for the nearest tree, but I wasn't sure Trevor was up for climbing.

Without warning, the music finally stopped and so did the attack. The mob lost interest in Trevor immediately. It was like a switch had been turned off. Within minutes, the concert-goers were back to sitting on the grass, hanging out, and tossing Frisbees.

I helped Trevor down. He was limping, and a large bruise had formed under his eye from where a soda can had hit him.

"What was that all about?" he said.

"I don't know," I said. "But I'm going to find out. Can you walk?"

He nodded and we headed to the car. Dominic caught up to us a few minutes later as I was unlocking the car door.

"Jessica, you're bleeding," he said. "I shouldn't have left you."

I looked down. There was a long scratch on my left arm. "I'm fine."

"Did you see where the music came from?" I asked him.

"No," he said. I followed the sound, but it stopped before I could get to the source. "But I found this." He held out a satin jacket that had HAMLIN embroidered on the back. I turned it over and saw the name on the front.

"I think the Pied Piper is Brett," I said.

Dominic didn't even ask any questions. "We're going to have to prove it. Let's get out of here."

CHAPTER NINETEEN

Side Effects May Vary wasn't on until seven, but everyone in the band had already squeezed into the assigned dressing room at the library, which I was pretty sure used to be a broom closet. Even though Jeff Cool wasn't performing, he was there — "for moral support," or so he said.

"You're going onstage like that?" Jeff's derisive comment was meant to shake my confidence and it did, almost as much as his sheer presence. He had no way of knowing that I couldn't wait for those broken arms of his to heal.

"Knock it off, Jeff," Dominic said. "I mean it."

"Is there something wrong with the way I look?" I wore black jeans and a faded band T-shirt. When I got dressed, I thought I was rockin' the whole understated thing.

Katrina threw something red and sparkly at me. "Here, put this on. You'll stand out in red."

I wasn't sure I wanted to stand out, but I took the

clothing and held it up. Red sequined pants. They looked impossibly small.

"Don't worry, they stretch," she assured me.

"They'd better," I said under my breath, and then went to the girls' bathroom to change. The band was pretty casual about changing in front of one another, but there was no way I was going to try to wiggle into those pants in front of Dominic. Or anyone else.

"What should I do with my hair?" I muttered. "Up or down?"

"Up," a voice behind me said. It was Sam. "Want some help?"

I whirled around and gave her a hug. "You made it!"

"Sean's here too," she said. "He's saving us seats up front. Now, about your hair."

"I don't know what to do with it," I admitted. "Or makeup. Katrina said I need to wear more so it will show up under the lights."

"We could do a bunch of different things. Your hair is so pretty."

"You mean red," I replied. "All the other girls in the family have that gorgeous strawberry blond hair and I got stuck with this."

"This," she said, holding up a handful of my hair, "is hair that people would kill for."

"Don't say that," I said, sitting down in a chair so

Sam could get to my hair more easily. "You have five minutes."

"I could do more if I had my flat iron or curler," she said. She took a comb and some hair spray from her purse and did some major hair tweaking. She finally let me look. She'd braided the long strands of hair framing my face and wrapped them up and around into a cool twisty hairdo.

"It's perfect!"

"Now hold still while I do your makeup," she said.

She whipped out a makeup bag and proceeded to apply eyeliner with the skill of a professional.

"Thanks, Sam," I said. "I've got to go! See you after the show."

I needed a minute to calm my nerves. At least I looked good, thanks to Sam.

I joined the rest of the band.

"Still no Vinnie," Katrina said grimly.

Just then, there was a knock on our dressing room door. I opened it and greeted Harmony, who was carrying a pair of drumsticks.

"Am I late?" she asked.

"Not at all," I said. I explained to the rest of the band that Harmony had agreed to be on standby, just in case Vinnie didn't show.

"It's not going to work," Jeff said dismissively.

"Shut up, Jeff," Dominic growled. "Do you have any better ideas?"

"She plays a bunch of instruments," I said. "She's a musical genius. Only she can't — " I stopped, unsure how to put it.

"I can't sing," Harmony said from the doorway. "But I can play."

"Thanks for helping out," Katrina said graciously.

"Are you ready?" Dominic asked.

"As ready as I'll ever be," I said.

"She looks ready to throw up," Jeff said. "Better get the barf bag ready."

Suddenly, I did feel like throwing up. I rushed outside, but the sound of his laughter followed me.

The crowd was much larger than any we had played for before. "I can't do this," I moaned.

Dominic had followed me out. He put a comforting hand on my shoulder. "Sure you can."

"Don't you dare tell me to picture the audience naked," I told him. "My parents are out there."

He laughed. "I was going to say picture one person to sing to and focus on his or her face. Pretend that person is the only one in the room."

The nausea receded. "Who do you picture?" I asked

impulsively. His face clouded and I added, "Never mind. You don't have to tell me."

"I always picture your face," he said.

I smiled at him. "Really?"

"Yes," he said. "Always."

Our eyes locked and neither of us looked away.

"We're on," Katrina said. "Are you two ready?"

I nodded. The announcer's voice seemed to come from far away. "Please welcome Side Effects May Vary."

Dominic gave me a reassuring smile before we took the stage. I looked out at the crowd, but I couldn't focus or find that face to calm me down.

My brother Sean let out a whistle I'd recognize anywhere. The first note rang out and I realized I was supposed to play along. I took a deep breath and gripped my pick tightly as I strummed.

I managed not to hyperventilate during the first two songs, but then it was time for me to actually sing the duet with Dominic. The band had voted to sing the acoustic version of "Stop Draggin' My Heart Around" at our last performance. We'd practiced some basic choreography, but it went completely out of my brain. Dominic caught my panicked look and crossed to where I stood, still holding the mike.

I finally remembered the words and the notes. Neither of us looked at the crowd once, which might not have been very exciting for them, but it made my heart beat faster.

After it was all over, I noticed that Ryan and Daisy were in the audience.

"I'll be right back," I said.

"I had no idea you were so talented," Daisy said when I approached them. "I knew you could play the guitar, but you have a beautiful voice."

"Jessica, you were amazing," Ryan said.

I blushed. My crush hadn't entirely faded, despite my feelings for Dominic. "Um, Ryan, I wanted to ask your advice."

"Everything okay?" Ryan asked.

"It's not for me," I said. "It's for a friend."

"I'll let you talk," Daisy said. "Ryan, see you at the house. Sean and Sam are coming over too."

He gave her a lingering kiss goodbye and I turned away.

After Daisy left, I said, "I think my friend is . . . like you, and I need to know how to help him."

"Like me how?" Ryan said. "Tall, with green eyes?"

I started stammering all over the place, but he stopped me with a smile. "I was just kidding," he said. "You have a friend who gets furry?"

"I think so," I said. "He hasn't exactly told me anything yet."

"Then what makes you think he's a werewolf?" Ryan asked.

"He's been moody," I said. "And he's bulked up quite a bit. Not as much as Sean did, but a lot."

"How old is he?"

"I'm not sure," I said. "He's a sophomore."

"Do you mean him? The lead singer?" Ryan asked. He gestured toward someone behind me.

I turned and saw Dominic. "No!" I said. "I think he has more in common with Daisy, psychically speaking. I'm talking about Connor Archer."

"Connor?" Ryan said. "I know his brother. I'll talk to him."

"Thanks, Ryan," I said. "I think he could use a friend who has already been through it."

"Gotta go," he said. "But we'll see you tomorrow morning."

That's when the judges were going to announce the finalists. And immediately after that, the bands who had made the cut would be performing to determine who would win the grand prize.

CHAPTER TWENTY

I awoke in a panic early on Sunday, afraid that I'd overslept and missed the announcement, but the clock on my nightstand reassured me.

Dominic had offered to give me a ride to the park, so I got ready, grabbed my guitar, and waited for him on the front porch.

As I sat there, I spotted a tiny figure making his way across the window ledge. I scooped him up before he could protest.

"Prince Humphrey," I said. "Princess Antonia has been worried sick about you."

He snorted. "The only person Her Royal Highness worries about is herself."

"She's been distraught," I said.

"I have spent an eternity with her," he said. "She is a spoiled little girl."

"What's your plan then?" I asked.

"I will seek my fortune in a new land," he said grandly. But he didn't sound too happy about it.

Dominic's car pulled into my driveway. I didn't have time to mediate a lovers' tiff, so I ran inside and then tiptoed into Katie's room. I placed the prince into his bedroom. "Think about it," I whispered. "She's not so bad."

I'd deal with them later. Dominic was waiting.

I slid my guitar into the trunk of his car and then we were on our way.

"Nervous?" Dominic asked.

"Yes, definitely," I said.

When we got to the park, I was happy to see that many of my friends in Nightshade had come out to support Side Effects May Vary. My parents and sisters arrived, all carrying signs. The Giordano girls and their boyfriends, with the exception of Poppy's guy, who didn't do sunlight, were in the audience too. Mr. and Mrs. Giordano were holding hands in the back. Raven and Andy waved from the front row.

Teddie Myles made the announcement. "The envelope, please," she said. A brief pause and then, "The finalists for the first annual Battle of the Bands are Drew Barrymore's Boyfriends, Hamlin, and Side Effects May Vary. The bands will be performing in that order, beginning in approximately one hour."

My dad let out a loud whoop and then everyone applauded.

Before we played, I ran into Selena. "Sorry you guys didn't make it," I said. "You were good."

"We'll play again one of these days, don't worry." Selena smiled. "Burning the sheet music was smart," she said. "I should have thought of it earlier. Harmony wouldn't have had to go through so much pain if I'd just—"

"None of us knew what to do," I said. "Don't beat yourself up over it."

"Thanks, Jessica. And if you decide not to join Side Effects May Vary, give us a call," she said. "We'd love to have you as our lead singer."

Me? A lead singer?

Dominic came up and heard the last part of the conversation. "Trying to steal her away from me, Selena?"

She gave him a cryptic look. "Not from you, just from the band."

"Want to watch Drew Barrymore's Boyfriends?" Dominic asked. "We're last and I don't feel like being cooped up in a dressing room."

After DBBF's first song, I said, "They're amazing. Trevor looks pretty good, considering he was attacked by an angry mob yesterday."

The band's set ended and then it was Hamlin's turn. "Wanna stay?" Dominic asked.

"Might as well," I said. "At least as long as I can take it."

Teddie then introduced Hamlin and I looked around.

"There aren't as many of their fans here as normal," Dominic said.

"That's because a bunch of them are locked up," I said. "Or at least I hope they are." I told him what had happened to Slim's.

There was a loud screeching sound as Brett sang too close to the microphone. I wasn't sure which noise hurt my ears more, the feedback or his singing.

Whatever magical hold Brett had over his fans was gone. There were cries of disbelief and one girl even held her hands over her ears. A couple of people took off their Hamlin tees and turned them inside out before putting them back on so the band's name was hidden from view.

Before the song even ended, Brett threw his guitar down and stomped offstage. "I'll dazzle them at the encore," he said. "As soon as I find that guitar."

But there wasn't an encore. Side Effects May Vary played next. We did all of our best-loved covers and Dominic wasn't interrupted by premonitions once. It was an incredible set.

Afterward, Teddie went onstage. "The winner for the

first annual Nightshade Battle of the Bands is . . . Side Effects May Vary!"

Dominic picked me up and twirled me around. As he put me back on the ground, I did something neither of us expected. I kissed him.

The next thing I heard was the sound of clapping. "You'd better get up there," someone advised us.

Dominic grabbed my hand and we walked onstage.

Teddie handed Katrina an oversized check and she held it in the air and grinned.

As the applause died down, Brett stormed onstage. "You're going to regret this," he shouted. He'd obviously found his guitar. He started to play softly, but even then, I could tell he was mangling the chords. There was a strange squeaking noise coming from somewhere.

At first I thought it came from his guitar, but then I realized it was something else. A dark blob appeared on the street. The louder Brett played, the bigger it became until it came close enough that I could see it wasn't a dark blob at all. It was hundreds of rats, streaming into the park.

"Smash his guitar!" I yelled to Dominic, who stood next to Brett.

"What?" he asked. It was hard to hear above the squealing.

"Smash it," I said, but he still didn't hear me.

I ran over and yanked the guitar out of Brett's hands and then took it by one end and smashed it on the ground. The music stopped, but the rats kept coming.

"It's not him," I yelled.

"No, it's me," Mitch Peverell said. He walked through the crowd, holding a flute, one that looked very familiar. He walked toward us and brought the flute to his lips.

I had to do something.

"You stole the flute, Mr. Peverell," I accused him. "And you used it to off the competition. You even killed Mr. Lindquist."

"Finally caught on, did you?" He snarled. "Unfortunately, it's much too late, at least for the city of Nightshade."

My stomach dropped at the thought that Flo could be trapped, or worse, in a cave somewhere like Scotty thanks to this guy. I needed to keep him talking. "Why are you so obsessed with convincing everyone how great Hamlin is?"

"Hey!" said Brett. "We are great."

Mr. Peverell whirled around. "Not until you had me and those magical instruments," he said. Brett looked genuinely hurt.

"But why?" Dominic asked. "You wanted Hamlin to win the competition so badly that you hurt the other musicians."

"Of course," he said. "Brett's my son. He deserves to be a star."

"What?" Brett cried. He dropped his guitar. "But my father is —"

"Me," Mr. Peverell said. "I know I left you years ago, Brett. But helping your band become famous was my way of making it up to you."

Brett sulked. "You're more interested in the band's money than being my dad."

Mr. Peverell didn't answer. Instead, he put the flute to his lips. The first note brought blood-freezing terror. I was unable to move, enchanted by the sound, yet frightened of it. The melody was both hauntingly beautiful and ominous.

"Cover your ears!" I yelled. But it was too late. The listeners were mesmerized. Blank looks appeared on their faces and they formed a single line behind Mr. Peverell, the Piper.

"We have to stop him," I said.

Brett was too mad to listen, or maybe it was a hereditary thing, but the music didn't affect him at all. He stepped in front of his father. "You owe me an explanation," he demanded.

"I don't have time for your star attitude right now," Mr. Peverell said. He was focused on Brett. It was my chance. I grabbed the flute and pulled, using all my virago strength.

I wrenched it out of his grasp. I knew what I had to do. It was a beautiful flute, but it was as evil as the man who played it. I held it up like a baseball bat and swung it against a tree. It made a dull thump, but didn't come apart. I swung again and this time it broke into pieces.

"No!" The Piper shoved me aside and dropped to his knees beside the useless instrument. The spell was finally broken.

Raven and Andy hauled the Piper up by his elbows and marched him over to Chief Wells, who looked dazed, but coherent. The chief cuffed him and read him his rights. She handed him over to Officer Denton and then crossed to where I stood.

"I was wrong about you, Jessica," Chief Wells said. "Teddie is right. You are special."

It made me feel all squirmy to get such recognition, but I was glad she'd decided I wasn't a troublemaker.

"Where is she?" Slim asked Mr. Peverell. "Where's Flo?"

"And Vinnie?" added Katrina, glaring at Brett.

"Dad, where are they?" Brett asked. "Tell me."

"Why should I?" Mr. Peverell sounded like a petulant child.

"Because I'm your son and it's the only thing I've ever asked of you," Brett said.

I finally caught a glimmer of something. Maybe a tiny bit of understanding about why Katrina found Brett the least bit attractive.

"I don't know," Mr. Peverell said. "Your friends must have skipped town. Musicians can be so unreliable." With that, he was taken away in the squad car.

CHAPTER TWENTY-ONE

We convened at Slim's. The mood was somber. Natalie put a comforting arm around Slim.

I looked around, expecting to see a trashed restaurant, but the place was spotless. Even the smashed window had been replaced.

"You guys cleaned up already," Dominic said. "We were going to help you."

"Not us," Slim said. "Circe Silvertongue and her niece came by and did their magic."

"That was such a nice surprise," Natalie said.

"You think everyone is as wonderful as you are, my love," Slim said fondly.

Maybe Selena had changed. She'd been so worried about Harmony and then she'd helped Slim and Natalie.

The diner phone rang and Slim answered it. "We're closed."

Instead of hanging up, he listened for a minute. "Florence Jane, where have you been? We've all been worried sick."

"It's Flo!" Raven cried.

"Shh, what's he saying?" Andy asked.

Slim said, "Vegas? What was Vinnie doing in Vegas?"

After a few minutes, he said goodbye and hung up. "She's okay!" he said. The space where his face should be was lit with a rosy glow. For a second, I caught a glimpse of what the non-invisible Slim would look like. But then that vision disappeared as quickly as it came.

"Flo called from the road. They will be home in a few hours. She and Vinnie are both safe."

"What happened?" Natalie asked.

"Apparently, before he went missing, Vinnie went out for a drink with Mitch Peverell. That's the last thing he remembers until he woke up in Vegas with no ID and no money."

"Mitch drugged him," Natalie said.

"That's what they think," Slim replied. "And then put him on the bus to Vegas. Vinnie woke up at the depot with no memory of how he got there."

"Sabotage," Raven said.

I nodded. "Mitch Peverell would do anything to make sure Hamlin won the Battle of the Bands, even playing dirty."

"Good work, Jessica," Slim said. "I'm glad they put him away."

"Flo's not going to be happy to hear about who else they put away," I said. "Her friend Hunter Verrat was involved in some nasty stuff. He was stealing magical items from Natalie's house."

"She won't be easy to convince," Slim admitted. "Are you sure?"

I nodded. "Officer Denton already made the arrest."

"Then he's safer in jail," Slim said. "Florence doesn't have many friends, and those she has, she trusts with her life."

"We're her friends," Raven said loyally.

"Hungry friends, I'm guessing," Slim said. "That's my cue to whip up some grub."

Our mood had lightened considerably now that we knew Vinnie and Flo were safe.

Natalie brought pitchers of soda to the table while Slim headed to the kitchen. Connor came over and tapped me on the shoulder.

"Jessica, can I talk to you? In private?" he said.

"I'll get the food," Dominic said. "Find me when you're done."

We went outside and walked a little distance before Connor burst out, "I'm not a werewolf."

"You're not?" I said. "But what about the new muscles?"

He looked startled. "Protein shakes," he said. "I wanted to try out for football next year."

"I feel so stupid," I said. "And then I asked Ryan to talk to you. I'm so sorry."

"Don't be," he replied. "Actually, Ryan was a big help. Remember how rude I was that night on the beach?"

I nodded.

"I saw something," he said. He lowered his voice. "I saw Mitch Peverell leading Scotty into the water using that flute. I wasn't sure what was happening, but I knew it wasn't good. I didn't want to believe it, especially because Mr. Peverell had expressed interest in Magic and Moonlight and I didn't want to think he was a bad guy. I was freaked out and didn't know who to tell. I finally told Ryan and he let the chief know. She asked me some questions, but Ryan stayed with me the whole time.

"I promised the chief I wouldn't say anything before, but he's already been arrested," Connor said. "I saw Mitch Peverell put Scotty's body in the cave."

"That's why you were acting so weird," I said.

He nodded. He stirred and said, "Take care of yourself, Jessica."

"I will," I promised. "You, too."

After he left, I went back into the diner and found Dominic.

"Everything okay?" he asked.

"Everything is fine," I said. "Although I mistakenly assumed Connor was a werewolf. That's why he wanted to talk to me."

"I thought he wanted to ask you out again or something," Dominic said.

"Of course not," I said. "Didn't you know? He's dating Selena."

He grinned. "That's the best news I've heard all day. For them, I mean."

Something was crawling up my arm. I lifted it up to check and met the irritated gaze of the dollhouse princess.

"How did you get here?" I asked.

"I am a princess," she said. "I can do anything. I seek my prince."

The rest of the castle inhabitants were on the floor, looking like tiny ants. The princess clung to my arm as I rescued her entourage.

There was a shriek and then Natalie came out of the kitchen holding a tiny prince in the palm of her hand.

"I've found my prince," she said wryly. "Swimming in my cup of coffee. But could someone explain this?"

She put the prince on the table and I did the same with the princess.

"With everything else going on," I said, "I completely forgot about the magical dollhouse. You see, I found this wishing powder in the attic and made a wish without realizing it. And then *this* happened." Flo had taken the inhabitants back here to the diner. They must have gotten out.

I looked down and saw the tiny prince and princess embracing passionately.

"What should we do?" I asked. "I don't think they can live at my house, but Katie would be heartbroken if I made her give up the dollhouse."

There was silence while we thought about our predicament. Natalie snapped her fingers. "Katie can keep the dollhouse," she said. "I'll make a duplicate and they can live in the spare bedroom."

"You can do that?" I asked.

"I'm a witch, remember?"

"Can I talk to you for a minute?" Dominic asked. "Outside?"

I followed him out. "What did you want to talk to me about?"

"This," he said. He drew me close and kissed me. It happened so quickly that I didn't have time to really enjoy it, so it was a good thing he did it again, only more slowly this time.

"What was that for?" I said when we separated.

"I've been an idiot," he said.

"I don't disagree with that," I said. "But go on."

"I want to get back together," he said. "No more cold feet, I promise."

He moved in to kiss me again, but I held out an arm to stop him. "You're going to have to do better than that, if you want to win me back."

"I do," he said. "More than anything. I'll prove it to you, I promise."

I nodded slowly. "I'll give it a try," I said. "But Dominic, this is your last chance."

"You won't regret it," he said. He put everything he had into his kiss. This time, I believed him.

Dominic and I still needed to talk about his concerns. I wanted to be absolutely sure that he wasn't going to change his mind again.

"I'm not going to stop being a virago," I told him, point-blank.

He looked incredulous. "I know that."

"You're not worried?"

"You've got to be kidding me," he said. "I just saw you take out a dude with a guitar. I'm not worried that you'll get hurt. I'm more worried about the other guy."

I laughed. "I guess I'm willing to try again, if you are."

"There you two are," Raven interrupted. "Dominic, I've been looking for you everywhere."

"What's going on?" he asked.

"Flo just got back from Vegas. And guess who she brought with her?"

"Her husband?" Dominic said dryly.

"Nope. She did bring Vinnie, but there's someone else, too," Raven said. There was a big smile on her face. "Mom's here, Dom. She's finally home."

"Okay," he said slowly. His face darkened. I gave him a concerned glance and he squeezed my shoulder reassuringly. "Jessica and I have some things to talk about, but I'll be home in a little bit, Raven," he finally said.

"Dominic, don't be like that," Raven said.

"I'm not," he said. "I just really want to talk to Jessica right now. Mom's been gone for two years. She can wait a few more minutes."

"But you're coming?" Raven asked.

"I promise we'll be there," he said. "I just want a few minutes alone with my girlfriend."

Raven grinned even wider. "Girlfriend, huh? It's about time."

We were quiet after she left. Finally, Dominic said, "So what do you think?"

"About Flo's elopement?"

"No." He laughed. "About being my girlfriend."

"Are you asking me?"

"I am," he replied.

"Then yes," I said. "My answer is yes."

He kissed me slowly and then hauled me to my feet. "C'mon, Jessica," he said. "There's someone I want you to meet."

Another strange day in Nightshade. I couldn't wait to see what would happen next.

Acknowledgments

Thanks to my editor Julie Tibbott, whose sharp eyes catch my goofs every time. Big appreciation to everyone at Houghton Mifflin Harcourt and my agent, Stephen Barbara. Special thanks to my family, who survives on takeout without complaint when I'm on deadline, and to my husband, who scares away all my technology gremlins.

Marlene Perez is the author of *The Comeback*, *Love in the Corner Pocket*, and the seven books in the Dead Is series, including *Dead Is the New Black*, which was named an ALA Quick Pick for Reluctant Young Adult Readers. She lives in Orange County, California, with her family. She loves music and sings regularly with top bands — loudly and out of tune in the shower.

www.marleneperez.com

How well do you know the **Dead Is** series?

Take this quiz to find out!

1. How many siblings does Jessica have?

a. two

b. twelve

c. five

d. seven

2. What does Dominic give Jessica as a birthday present?

a. a necklace

b. a guitar

c. flowers

d. a magic flute

3. What is the name of Eva's favorite actor?

a. Vincent Price

b. George Clooney

c. Johnny Depp

d. Robert Pattinson

4. Which of these Nightshade residents had a cooking show?

a. Flo

b. Slim

c. Circe

d. Daisy

5. For which birthday did Jessica's family throw her a surprise party?

a. twelfth

b. thirteenth

c. fifteenth

d. sixteenth

6. Which of these songs has Dominic never sang?

a. "Evil Woman"

b. "Promises, Promises"

c. "Love Potion Number Nine"

d. "Killer Queen"

7. Who owns the Black Opal?

a. Ms. Minerva

b. Teddie Myles

c. Nicholas Bone

d. Officer Denton

8. Jessica's tattoo is in what shape?

a. a rose

b. cabbage

c. a unicorn

d. a whirlwind

9. What kind of pet does Eva have?

a. a bulldog named Fluffy

b. a rabbit named Bunnicula

c. a raven named Poe

d. a cat named Midnight

10. Selena lives across the street from

a. the Mason house

b. the Wilder Mansion

c. Slim's Diner

d. Nightshade High School

11. Which one of these guys tends to get a little furry when there's a full moon?

a. Connor

b. Ryan

c. Dominic

d. Vinnie

12. The original Black Opal was destroyed on what night?

a. Grad Night

b. prom night

c. the night before Christmas

d. the night of the living dead

13. Jessica and Connor share the same

a. dentist

b. guitar teacher

c. milkshake

d. hair color

14. Which one of these characters was never the new kid in Nightshade?

a. Raven

b. Selena

c. Edgar Love

d. Daisy

15. What color did Edgar Love's followers wear?

a. black

b. hot pink

c. purple

d. yellow

16. Which virago is a pacifist?

a. Flo

b. Raven

c. Jessica

d. Andy

17. Andy predicts that Flo will retire from being a virago when she gets

a. injured

b. relocated

c. married

d. fed up with Jessica

18. Which one of these characters attends UC Nightshade?

a. Samantha

b. Sean

c. Ryan

d. Natalie

19. Which one of these characters lives with both of his or her parents?

a. Dominic

b. Jessica

c. Andy

d. Samantha

20. Which sports team are Jessican and Eva on?

a. soccer

b. softball

c. basketball

d. track and field

Answers:

1. d.; 2. b.; 3. a.; 4. c.; 5. c.; 6. a.; 7. b.; 8. d.; 9. c.; 10. a.;
11. b.; 12. a.; 13. b.; 14. d.; 15. c.; 16. b.; 17. c.; 18. a.; 19.
b.; 20. a.

How did you do?

1–5 correct answers: New kid in town.

6–10: You can pass for a local, but you might be a norm.

11–15: Virago-in-training or magical possibilities.

16–20: Honorary Nightshade resident.